THE BILLIONAIRE CLUB

GETAWAY BAY RESORT ROMANCE, BOOK 5

ELANA JOHNSON

ISBN-13: 978-1-63876-014-6

ONE

LEXIE KELLER SAT at the vanity, applying her makeup in quick swooshes of the brush to properly contour her face. Some women were blessed with high cheekbones and a porcelain complexion, but Lexie took classes and spent enormous amounts of money to achieve those things on the daily.

Or at least the appearance of them.

As her fortieth birthday approached, she couldn't help feeling a little melancholy. She pushed the feelings away and swiped on a generous amount of the sparkly, razzle-dazzle lip gloss Sasha had given her for Christmas a few months ago.

Sasha Redding had come into Lexie's life quite unexpectedly, and through Jasper Rosequist of all people.

Still, her part-time job at The Straw now provided Lexie with the one bright ray of hope in her life—and how pathetic was that? And she thought she'd been boring as a penny pusher, a number lover, and a mutual fund heiress.

But the moment she stepped into The Straw, she felt lighter than she ever had. "Hey, girl," she said to Sasha, who was bent over a notebook at the back counter.

"Lex, how are you?"

"Doing great." Lexie had become an expert fibber over the years. *Why did you come to the island? Work. Are you seeing anyone, dear? Yeah, Mom, I see men all the time.*

No one had to know that yes, Lexie worked here on the island, but she could work from anywhere. And her mom didn't need to know that the men she saw were fellow Nine-0 Club members who had zero romantic interest in her. And she wasn't interested in any of them.

"Brewing up something new?" she asked Sasha. The owner of the drink stand, Sasha had an incredible palette and an adventurous imagination when it came to fruits and flavorings.

"Maybe," she said, pressing the eraser end of her pencil against her temple. "I can't quite make it come together. But I think something for spring would be nice. Get our customers back in here after this dreary winter."

The rainy season had been bad this year, and Lexie immediately thought about the people who'd been stranded up in the mountains after the landslides just after the new year. Thankfully, everyone had made it home safely, and Lexie had just read about one couple who'd met on the excursion, fell in love while they were stuck in a remote shack, and were now engaged.

So it proved that people could meet under the most

extraordinary of circumstances, and Lexie hadn't felt so foolish for thinking her one and only was going to come through the line at The Straw one day.

She tied an apron around her waist and faced the front of the building where the order window was. No one waited for a drink, and she asked, "How long has it been dead?"

"Only about ten minutes." Sasha seemed really distracted. "You'll be okay if I run out for a few minutes? I need to go pick up the Sunrise Special cards and take them over to Sweet Breeze."

Lexie opened her mouth to offer to take them later that evening, when she'd be in the owner's penthouse for her Nine-0 meeting. But the group was exclusive, and secret, and Lexie snapped her lips closed again.

"I'll be fine," she said instead and scraped her thick, dark hair into a ponytail on the very tippy top of her head. Sasha left without saying anything, her focus still on the notebook as she made her way up to the sidewalk to her car.

A couple appeared then, and Lexie put on her business face, one that wore a smile and did mental math and enjoyed being around other human beings.

For a while there, when she'd first come to the island, Lexie was sure she could be happy living in her spacious rambler, anonymously, on the south side of the island. But she hadn't been.

"Lemon Whip," she repeated. "And Berry Blast. That's eleven ninety-two." The couple paid, and she blended, and a line formed. Lexie kept her focus on what was immediately in front of her, but that didn't mean the dark-haired man loitering along the beachwalk, by the biggest palm, didn't catch her attention.

Of course he did, as it wasn't the first time Lexie had seen him in that exact position, leaning against the tree with one shoulder, both hands in the pockets of his shorts, one foot crossed over the other at the ankle.

Jason Burnes.

If he thought for one moment she didn't see him when he spied on her, he was wrong. Her mouth filled with a sour taste that had nothing to do with the limes she'd just zested.

Jason had come to the island over a year ago, when Tyler Rigby—a fellow billionaire in Hawaii—had made up a fake engagement. Tyler and everyone else on the island knew Jason as a reporter for a poker magazine.

But Lexie knew him as a bartender in New York City, where she'd lived before making her big move across the ocean and leaving her high-rise life behind—and the dangerous, abusive ex-fiancé that had ruined her so completely she hadn't been able to stay in a city of millions with him still there.

When Lexie finished with the customers, she stood very still in the window, shooting her best laser gaze toward where Jason leaned against the tree. Almost a challenge. *Like, Well? What are you doing here again?*

He ducked behind the trunk, and a measure of satisfaction pulled through her. She'd never confronted him so fully before, and though thirty yards separated them, she felt a bit breathless and weak.

Why was he watching her? And why couldn't she just let it go, like she had all the other times?

Sasha returned, asking, "How'd it go?" and Lexie snatched up the washcloth and started wiping the counter. She knew one of Sasha's pet peeves was a sticky, drippy service station.

"Great." She wiped in circles, her eyes drifting back to that palm tree as worry gnawed at her insides.

That evening, Lexie straightened her blouse and patted her hair as Sterling, the valet at Sweet Breeze, got behind the wheel of her car. She loved coming to the Nine-0 meetings, and she'd held them at her house a time or two. They'd gotten a couple of new additions over the past six months, and Lexie had enjoyed making friends with the new women on the island.

But she wasn't as business minded as most in the club, though none of them knew it. Sure, she knew what went on at Keller Investments, the huge financial resources company where she owned fifty-one-percent of the shares. But her oldest brother, Luke, was the one who really ran things from their thirty-five-story building in New York, and her youngest brother, Bruce, was the CFO.

So her CEO was really in title only. Still, she had the right number of zeroes in her bank account, and no one really seemed to care what she did if she had that.

The lobby at Sweet Breeze seemed unusually quiet, though she supposed for a Wednesday at almost nine p.m., there wouldn't be much going on at the luxury resort.

She stepped past the public elevators and down a hall

that led to Fisher's private one and pushed the button. The light flashed red, and she keyed in the code.

"Four-seven-six-two," a man said, and Lexie practically leapt away from him. She hadn't heard him coming, and her heartbeat rippled like a flag in a stiff breeze as she took in his tall frame, wide shoulders, dark hair, and the soapy, spicy scent of his cologne.

Jason Burnes.

"Are you following me?" she demanded, wishing the car wasn't already up on the blasted twenty-eighth floor. She really had to get away from this man.

"Not at all."

She cocked her hip, wishing his voice didn't reach right down into her stomach and make it vibrate in a good way. "Right. I saw you at the beach today." *And every other day I work,* she thought but kept to herself.

"It's a public beach." His dark eyes that had once consumed her so completely while she sipped seltzer water flashed, and she recognized the danger in them. She didn't trust journalists, especially ones who came to the trade after five other attempts at a career in wildly different fields. So her money could buy her some information, something she didn't go around flaunting but which she also didn't ignore.

"What do you want?"

Surprise lifted his eyebrows, and a softness she hadn't expected entered his eyes. "How's Luke?"

"Better now that you're gone." The elevator chimed and the doors started to slide open. She stepped inside, intending to leave without another word. The likes of Jason Burnes didn't deserve a *good-bye* or a *nice to see you*. Because she wasn't glad to see him.

And he'd gotten bolder, approaching her in this tiny hallway. Or maybe it only felt tiny because he was so big, so broad, and still so beautiful.

She shook her head as she punched at the only button in the elevator, the one that would take her to Fisher's penthouse.

"I didn't leak that story," he said. "I quit instead of talking to the reporters."

Their eyes locked, and Lexie wanted to believe him so, so badly. Her heart thundered like water roaring over cliffs.

"Lex." The agony in his voice wasn't hard to hear, but Lexie only lifted her chin, determined not to show him that she still had feelings for him.

The car doors slid shut, removing the handsome face of the only man Lexie Keller had ever truly loved from her sight. The elevator moved, and Lexie slumped against the back wall.

It was ridiculous how easily he could remove her every defense. How her hopes skyrocketed just from the nearness of him. That her feelings, though seven years old, were still there, just dormant.

The elevator beeped again, opening to reveal Fisher's penthouse. Lexie smoothed her hair again and faced her future: making drinks to stay social during the day and attending secret meetings with her rich friends at night.

There was absolutely no room for Jason. Not again.

"You wanna come?" Gabi, one of the newer members of the Nine-0 Club, pulled her shirtsleeves down and looked at Lexie. "You can just have coffee."

Lexie smiled and nodded as she shouldered her purse. Gabriella Rossi was an old friend whose family had made their fortune in cruise ships. So she knew Lexie didn't drink much more than champagne, and even then she usually just held the glass so people wouldn't pester her about drinking more.

Her father had been an alcoholic, and a mean one. So while Lexie loved her parents, she didn't love what alcohol had done to her childhood.

"Are you okay?" Gabi put her hand on Lexie's elbow. "You've been distracted all night."

"It's...." Lexie met Gabi's lighter brown eyes, hers more the color of caramel while Lexie's were like black coffee. When Gabi had first come to Hawaii, Lexie had panicked. She didn't want anyone on the island who'd known her in her previous life. But everything had been fine, and Lexie had worried needlessly.

Maybe Jason would be like that.

No. She shook her head. "Another old friend has come to the island."

Gabi linked her hand through Lexie's arm. "Intriguing. Male or female?"

"Male."

Gabi nodded to Ira, who set his glass on the credenza and joined them as they walked out. She and Ira had started seeing each other about six weeks ago, and the atmosphere felt a bit awkward as the three of them loaded onto the elevator.

"Do I know him?" Gabi asked, always the lover of games, especially riddles and puzzles.

"I don't believe you do." Lexie had kept her relationship with Jason under wraps as much as possible. As her younger brother's best friend and a man way below her father's standards, Jason had agreed to keep their dates, hand-holding, and kissing behind closed doors.

She went to his place, or the bar, or they met somewhere at odd hours. He never came to her place, or picked her up, or pressed her against her front door and kissed her goodnight.

"You don't sound happy about him being here." Gabi stepped out of the elevator with Lexie, leaving Ira to follow along like a puppy.

"I'm not."

"Was he more than a friend?"

Yes. "No."

"Well, that doesn't give me much to go on. I assume you haven't mentioned him to me."

"No." They reached the front doors and Lexie paused, the scent of Jason's cologne hanging in the air. It took all of her self-control not to start swiveling her head back and forth to find him. "I'm not feeling up to coffee. I think I'm coming down with something. You two go on."

Plus, she didn't need to be the third wheel with Gabi and Ira when their relationship was so new. Perhaps she could call Sasha and see if they could grab a late night snack together.

But she and Jasper were together now, and Lexie stood in the brightly lit foyer, wishing she had someone to go home to as well. Drawing in a deep breath, she stepped out to the valet, expecting to see Sterling but coming face-to-face with Jason instead.

"What are you doing here?" she blurted even as she scanned him from head to toe and found him wearing the service clothes of someone who worked at Sweet Breeze.

"I work here," he said needlessly, his eyes devouring her too. She wished she didn't like it so much, crave his attention so strongly, or know exactly where to find him next time she wanted to see him.

He grinned at her as if he could hear all of her thoughts inside her mind. "Do you need your car?"

TWO

JASON COULD'VE JUST GRABBED Lexie's keys and retrieved her car. Taken his tip. And stood behind that stupid little podium for the rest of the night. He'd done exactly that for several weeks now—minus the running into Lexie part.

Not that he hadn't tried. He was *not* stalking her, but he'd noticed she came to Sweet Breeze quite often. Used that swanky private elevator down the hall away from the guest elevators. Disappeared up to the owner's penthouse for hours and then came out in the dead of night.

And she wasn't the only one. Fisher DuPont definitely had something going on up on that twenty-eighth floor, and it involved Getaway Bay's wealthiest men and women.

But the stars hadn't aligned until tonight, and someone else had always been working when Lexie came to Sweet Breeze.

His hand twitched toward hers like he might touch her. But from the burning look on her face, he'd be incinerated if he did. "Want to go for a ride?" he asked instead, actually shifting one foot back and leaning his weight onto it, expanding the distance between them.

Her eyebrows went up, and her dark, almost black, eyes searched his. "A ride? Aren't you working?"

"Oh, come on." He chuckled like he took joyrides every time he worked. Which he didn't. He gestured to the key rack behind the podium. "There's just you waiting for your car."

"How long have you been waiting?" she asked.

"I work here," he said, as if the monkey suit he wore wasn't enough evidence. He didn't particularly mind the job. His insomnia kept him up most nights, and this way, he made a bit of cash. Enough to pay for a little cottage on the beach, where he could watch the sun rise and swim in the bay before anyone else even got up.

"Yes, you and your revolving career."

Jason kept his mouth shut, because he had no argument. So he was a Jack-of-All-Trades. It wasn't a crime. Could he help it if he got bored easily? Or if he was really good at picking up new skills? Or that he wanted to be close to Lexie, maybe see if they could rekindle what they'd had in New York?

He almost shook his head to get that last thought out of his head. She was not why he'd come to Hawaii—that had been to get a story for a magazine, the job he'd had before this one. But he'd loved Hawaii, and when Aces High announced they were downsizing, he made their job easier by resigning.

He was tired of writing articles about poker anyway.

And he'd come back to Hawaii, right here to Getaway Bay, because he'd felt something here he hadn't anywhere else. He still wasn't sure what it was, and at the moment, all he could feel was the weight and sharpness of Lexie's glare.

"So?" He stepped toward the pegboard and took down her keys. "Just a quick ride." He sensed her wavering, because the woman loved driving at night, under the stars, when no one else was awake.

At least she had when they were dating in New York. And they'd had to go pretty far outside the city to get a dark enough sky to see the stars.

"You'll lose your job," she said.

"I'll find another one."

She snorted, but Jason felt very near victory. She hadn't even gotten close to the word no yet.

"This pays your bills?"

"How about I tell you about it while we drive around the island? Just over to the volcano fields and back. Thirty minutes, tops." He jangled the keys. "It's really dark out there tonight. Loads of stars. And you have a convertible." He added a smile to his statement, his memory suddenly bringing forth something she'd told him in his office at the bar in New York.

Your smile makes me want to kiss you.

He hoped it still did. The way her eyes dropped to his mouth might be a good indicator that she was reliving the same memory.

"I'm tired," she said.

"An excuse," he shot back. "Heard that one lots of times."

"I bet you have." She folded her arms, and Jason didn't like that. He'd taken a class on body language during his brief stint as a police officer in Baltimore. Folded arms meant closed off. Done talking. Holding something back.

"All right," he said. "I'll get your car." He walked away, half-hoping she'd call him back. Or catch up to him and walk beside him. She did neither.

He got behind the wheel of her car, folding his long legs under the steering wheel before starting the ignition. Whoever had sold her this car had done a great job, because it didn't seem like the kind of car Lexie would like.

Black, sleek, convertible, leather seats, and a ton of horsepower under the hood. Felt like more Luke's style, and he wondered if her younger brother had bought her the car as a gift. No matter what, Jason liked driving it, even if it was ten miles per hour through a parking garage.

He pulled up to where she still stood on the curb, now swiping through something on her phone. She didn't even look up when he parked and got out. He dutifully moved the seat back, as had been drilled into him, and left one hand on the door frame so he could close it for her after she'd slid inside the vehicle.

She didn't move, and Jason had nothing better to do. He'd been watching a movie on his phone before the little meeting upstairs had broken up, but nothing was as interesting as Lexie Keller. Nothing ever had been, not for Jason.

His heart bumped extra hard for a beat, then steadied while he continued watching her. She finally looked up and walked over to him, wearing such different clothes from what she did at the drink stand where she worked.

Well, Jason was still trying to figure out if she actually got paid for her time there. He couldn't fathom why she'd volunteer to blend up frozen drinks, but she certainly didn't need the money.

Maybe she does, he thought, and not for the first time. So maybe he spent way too much time thinking about Lexie. Maybe he had been for seven long years.

"I'll give you twenty-five minutes." She tapped one perfectly manicured finger against his chest and walked past him and around the front of the car. He laughed when he noticed the extra sway in her hip and as she cocked one eyebrow before ducking into the passenger seat.

Jason cast one long look at the sliding glass doors that led into the foyer, knowing that Owen Church, the general manager, had left three hours ago. No one was scheduled to come in tonight, or else he'd have their name on a list, with the arrival time of their flight. Sweet Breeze operated at the highest levels of customer service, right down to the valet.

He could spare thirty minutes. No one would even know.

So he moved the seat back and got behind the wheel again. With the door closed, and one hand on the gear shift, he asked, "What made you change your mind?"

"Just drive, Jason." Lexie buckled her seat belt, and pulled her hair out of the tight ponytail it had been in all day. She shook her head, the waves and waves of dark hair tumbling over her shoulders and down her back.

Jason felt the silky ghost of it between his fingers, and every muscle in his body tightened and his mouth turned dry.

He pushed the button to lower the top and then put the

car in gear and got it going, thinking maybe he should just take her back to his place and see what else he could convince her to do. He'd never had to coax her into kissing him, but as he glanced right to check the non-existent traffic, he knew he'd have to do a lot of work to get out of her doghouse.

"Music?" he asked.

"Have we ever listened to music on our joyrides?"

Jason noted the plural pronouns of *we* and *our*, and they made him smile. He tried to hide it as he accelerated down the main streets and through all the green lights. Soon enough, they left Getaway Bay behind and were winding along the coast.

"It really is dark," she said. Her hair flew around her face as she tipped it toward the heavens, and Jason thought he'd never seen anything quite as angelic as Lexie Keller, at midnight, flying along the highway on a tropical island.

If someone had told Jason this morning this was what he'd be doing tonight, he would've scoffed and laughed and referred them to a psychiatrist. But things had changed the moment Lexie had stared him down from the drink stand. He didn't try to hide when he went by The Straw, but he also never went to order anything either.

Probably should have.

But then he'd have to talk, as well as formally reveal his presence on the island, and he hadn't wanted to do either of those.

Even now, he waited for her to say something. Jason was exceptionally good at waiting. His life as a private detective in Brooklyn had taught him that.

"How long do you plan on staying on the island?" Lexie asked.

"Indefinitely," he said. "I bought a place over in the other bay, right on the tip of the island."

"You know that area gets hit by every tropical storm that comes our way, right?"

Again with the plural pronoun. "It's kind of a dive already, so." He shrugged like he didn't care about losing his beachfront property. But just because it was a six-hundred-square-foot studio didn't mean he didn't love it.

"And you're a valet."

"And I work security at the hotel too," he said.

She made a small harrumphing noise that indicated her disapproval. He was actually surprised she hadn't seen him standing next to the lobby or over by the restaurant. But most people ignored a cop until they needed one. Walked right on by, their noses buried in their phones, or a conversation, or in Lexie's case, worrying over if her clothes were at ninety-degree angles.

He smiled just thinking about her perfectionism. The headlights flashed over the sign that said they would arrive at the volcano fields in only a mile. He gunned the engine, determined to cover that mile in only seconds.

Lexie squealed, her laughter lifting into the sky after that.

Jason grinned and laughed too. Achievement, unlocked. He'd learned early on that it took a lot to loosen the mutual fund heiress up, but once that was done, she'd be loyal and fun and sexy....

He slammed on the brakes, and Lexie's laughter got sucked into her throat as she braced herself. The car came to a stop only a few feet from the gated road that continued up to the park and the volcanic fields.

He'd explored them a couple of times already, and he found the rocky landscape as alien as it was beautiful.

His chest heaved with adrenaline, and he twisted to look at Lexie. She wore the excitement and wonder in her expression too, and relief combined with satisfaction inside him. She still had some of the Lexie he knew. Different, sure. Changed, absolutely. Better, definitely.

"It's beautiful here," she said, tearing her gaze away and focusing on the stars. She unbuckled her belt and climbed up to perch on the doorframe, her head tilted back to drink in the magnificence of the stars.

Jason usually did too, but only because he'd always wanted to see what she saw. He'd never quite been able to, and tonight, he didn't even try.

Tonight, he only wanted to drink in the slope of Lexie's neck, and the beauty in her face. And while he knew, absolutely, that he wouldn't be telling her all the nitty gritty details of his past, which meant they absolutely wouldn't be getting back together.

THREE

LEXIE WOKE THE NEXT MORNING, a smile on her face from the fantastic dream she'd been having. Jason had driven her car at high speeds through the night, the bright pinpoints of light above them reminding Lexie of how small she was, how wonderful the world could be.

Sometimes she lost sight of that, and nothing had ever grounded her as much as the stars, strange as that may seem.

She snuggled into the blankets, a little smile on her face. Then her eyes popped open. "That wasn't a dream." She sat up, her hair feeling like a nest on her head, and found the sun streaming through her bedroom window.

What time was it?

She reached for her phone. After nine o'clock. She couldn't believe she'd slept so long. Panic blipped through her as she saw all the notifications on her phone. It would be mid-afternoon in New York, and by the four texts from Luke, her brother had needed her.

She thought about Jason as her brother's line rang, and when he didn't answer, Lexie pushed herself out of bed. Hanging up without leaving a message, she tried to shake last night's midnight ride out of her head.

It wasn't something someone her age did, and she couldn't believe she'd given in to Jason's sly, charming smile. But when he'd asked her what made her change her mind, she certainly couldn't tell him that she didn't want to go home alone.

He'd probably suggest he come with her, his smile switching from coy to hungry in less than a second.

"That's not fair." Lexie stabbed at her phone again to dial Luke. The line only rang once before a text came from him. *Meeting. Give me 15*

She ended the call, her thoughts still lingering on the wrong man. But it wasn't fair to assume Jason would try to seduce her or get her to sleep with him. He'd never done that when they'd dated years ago, and she'd always set the pace of their intimacy. She couldn't imagine it would be any different this time.

Startled, she sucked in a breath. "There is no this time, Lex. Jeez." She set her phone on her nightstand and pulled on a pair of yoga pants and a tank top the color of the palm leaves that grew in her yard.

Luke's fifteen minutes would be at least thirty, so Lexie put on her sneakers and went into the backyard, calling, "Slinky. Brownie." She glanced around for the stray cats she'd adopted, and when she didn't see them, bent to pick up their bowls.

They wouldn't come in the house, and Lexie didn't really want them inside anyway. But they stayed around her property, and she fed them well and had even put out a waterproof doghouse with cat toys inside for when it rained.

Now that summer was here, she sometimes found the cats snoozing in the shade of the house. But today, they couldn't be found anywhere. She filled their food bowls and gave them fresh water, and then puttered around the yard.

She spent hours in her yard, making sure every flower, every tree, every shrub was healthy and pruned and thriving. She could have weddings in her yard and charge a lot of money for them. But she didn't have a lot of visitors over. Sasha and Jasper had come a few times. The Nine-0 Club members on occasion.

But mostly, Lexie's house and yard were a place of refuge for her, even if she didn't want to be there alone sometimes.

Her phone sounded, and she pulled it from the webbing on her outer thigh. But it wasn't Luke.

Sasha. *Some friends and I are sunning at the beach this morning. Want to join us?*

Lexie had seen her friend leave The Straw in the middle of the afternoon with a beach bag, trading out her work visor for a floppier, more festive sun hat. She'd never asked Sasha where she was going, because everyone deserved time off. In fact, it was why Lexie worked at the stand in the first place—to give Sasha a break.

All women. No talk of men, promise. Sasha had added a smiley face to the end of her message, and Lexie couldn't think of a reason not to go. She and Sasha had been friends for just over a year, and she'd never been invited to the beach. So what had changed?

Yeah, sure, Lexie typed. *Which beach?* She could sit in the sun and listen to women talk. She'd done worse things.

Right on the edge of Sweet Breeze's private beach.

Lexie could find that easily enough, and she went back inside to change and put a few things in a beach bag. She wasn't the type of woman to normally lie around in the sun, sipping a fruity drink while wearing oversized sunglasses. But she didn't hate it either.

As she got ready and drove around the curve in the island toward the huge hotel in the bigger of the two bays, she mused over the *no talk of men* promise. She'd mentioned to Sasha that her birthday was coming up and she'd like to meet a man, but it just didn't seem to be happening for her.

Sasha had asked a few questions, but Lexie had clammed up. Such conversations required a trip to the past, and Lexie had left that behind using a one-way ticket five years ago.

She'd just pulled into the public beach lot when her phone rang. "Luke," she said, all business now despite the flirty, fun, and fuchsia bikini she wore beneath a sheer cover up.

"Lex," he said. "Where were you this morning?"

"I was out late," she said. It wasn't that unusual for her to have late meetings, and Luke didn't question it. "What's going on?"

"One of our biggest clients has filed for bankruptcy." Luke sounded like he'd been awake for days, and Lexie pictured her younger brother—all six-foot-four-inches of him, slouched at a desk, rubbing his forehead the way he did when he was thinking too hard.

Everything about him was a shade lighter than her—his hair, his eyes, his skin. Of course, he spent twelve hours a day in an office building, and well, she lived in Hawaii.

"Which client?" she asked, already fearing the answer. If he said one of their real estate moguls....

"Bangerter Electronics."

Lexie breathed a sigh of relief. "Luke, electronic companies go in and out of business like it's breathing."

"Not this one."

"So what are we looking at?"

"Eight percent of our clients have investments in Bangerter."

"Well, pull them. Put their money somewhere else."

"All trading has been frozen."

Lexie stared past the line in front of Two Coconuts, wishing she were standing ankle-deep in the lapping waves as they came ashore. She wasn't even sure why she needed to know this. She didn't have control over any of the trading accounts. He didn't need her authorization for anything.

He just needed her support.

"What does Linus say?"

"He says as soon as the floor unfreezes, we're dumping Bangerter."

"He's not wrong."

"Who should we go with?"

And that was where Lexie came in. She spent her time on the beach, or her beautiful backyard, or in her club meetings learning about the best upstarts, the rising stars in the business world, who to invest in now to make the most money later.

She sorted through her memory. "Assuming the clients want to stay in electronics, there's Python Products."

"Python Products," Luke repeated, probably for the benefit of an assistant, who would look up the trading codes for the company. "We've been in touch with about eighty-five percent of the clients affected. Most are simply telling us to choose a new investment. Is that Python?"

"It'll outperform Bangerter," Lexie said. "But the best investment for those willing to risk is real estate." She couldn't believe she was saying it. The housing market crash of a few years ago had almost decimated their whole company. But it had been rebuilt, and commercial real estate was especially thriving.

"The kind where they buy in to a big property with a small amount of money." Luke wasn't asking. He knew the market well enough to know things like this. But Lexie was the research arm, and she sent him several emails each week with a list of companies for their low-risk, medium-risk, and high-risk investors.

"Yep."

A shadow appeared in her window, and she glanced up to see Jason standing there, miming for her to roll the glass down. "I have to go," she said. "Are we good?"

"Yes. Keep your phone nearby. I can text."

"Will do." Lexie hung up with her brother and took her time stowing her phone in her beach bag before she got out of the car.

Jason had backed up a few steps, and he scanned her

from her flip-flopped feet to her pathetic attempt at a beach hat. By the time his eyes came back to hers, Lexie felt like he'd set her skin on fire.

"Nice outfit," he said in an utterly bored voice.

Lexie knew he could see her swimming suit beneath the flimsy white cover up. She cocked her hip. "I'm going to the beach, not a board meeting."

He cocked his head at her, and she tried not to find it the sexiest movement a man had ever mad. "I didn't think you went to board meetings any more."

"I don't." She glanced over her shoulder. "This is a girls-only morning. Sorry." She took a couple of steps away, but Jason appeared at her side anyway.

"Is that so?" His fingers brushed hers as they walked, and Lexie tucked her rioting emotions behind a blank mask. She'd never been happier for her pair of sunglasses, and she spotted Sasha on the west side past Sweet Breeze's beach. She waved, and Lexie waggled her fingers back.

"So you're saying I can't be on this public beach?" This time, he moved his hand into her personal space and stroked his fingers down hers, a deliberate touch that wasn't entirely unwelcome. In fact, Lexie wanted to grab onto his hand and hold it. She could almost remember the shape of it in hers, the warmth from his skin, and taste of the caramel she'd once licked from—

Lexie jerked away from him physically, trying to shut off her brain. "I'm saying, I'm going to go sit by my friends, and I've been told it's a no-male zone, even in conversation." She strode away from him. Well, as much as she could actually stride in the squishy sand. It probably looked like she was waddling with the way her legs shook.

Being near Jason was a mistake. She could already feel herself allowing soft thoughts about him, mostly because she hadn't really known what had happened when everything came crashing down. So much had happened, that she hadn't been able to process it all.

His chuckle followed her down the beach, but he didn't physically join her. She arrived at the semi-circle of women and glanced around, taking in the familiar faces.

"Oh, you made it." Sasha jumped up from her beach chair and gave Lexie a quick hug. "Guys, this is Lexie. She works at my stand, you know?"

Lexie felt cold despite the mid-April sun. "You're Fisher's wife," she said to a redheaded woman. "Stacey, right?"

"That's right." She grinned at Lexie like she knew all of her secrets. Lexie trusted Fisher, but Stacey lived in his penthouse now that they were married, and while Lexie had never seen her there during a Nine-0 meeting, surely she knew what her husband was involved in.

Nothing nefarious. But definitely exclusive.

Like this beach club, she thought.

"And you married Marshall Robison over Christmas," she said to the power blonde who owned the premiere car service on the island. "Esther, I believe." It took a lot for Lexie to forget a name, and as Marshall and Fisher were like peanut butter and jelly, their wives were often around as a set too.

"And you're Tyler's wife, Tawny. And Jasper...." All of these men were in the Nine-0 Club. Had they told Sasha to invite Lexie? She turned to her friend. "Can I talk to you for a second?"

"Oh, don't do that." Stacey got up and took a few steps through the sand. She gave Lexie a hug too. "Sasha's been telling us about you, and we thought we'd invite you. Nothing more." She gave Lexie a warm smile and turned back to the group. "Right, ladies?"

"Right," Esther said. "Pull up a patch of sand. Winnie here was just telling us about her no-good, cheating ex who's gotten his latest girlfriend pregnant."

Lexie glanced at a Hawaiian woman who had the most beautiful hair she'd ever seen. "I'm so sorry."

"I'm not," Winnie said. "Serves him right." She took a long drink from her Styrofoam cup. "And I'm not looking to get married like these ladies."

"So she says," Tawny said, already leaning back in her chair, her face tilted toward the sun, and her eyes closed behind her sunglasses.

"And this is Gina Jackson," Sasha said. "She owns Classy Closets, and Stacey's just hired her to do all the rooms at Aloha Hideaway."

"There are five rooms," Stacey said as she lay back on her towel. "So it's not much."

"Sure it is," Gina said, pulling her obviously dyed hair into a high ponytail. She gave Lexie a winning smile. "I'm new too. Only been on the island for about a month."

And yet she was already in this club. Lexie couldn't help feel a bit stung, but she supposed Gina had gotten an invite because she was working with Stacey, same as Lexie worked with Sasha.

"So who was that dreamboat you were talking to?" Gina asked, casting her eyes toward the parking lot.

"Dreamboat?" Lexie snorted and shook her head. She spread out her towel, noting that she needed to get one of the beach chairs Sasha, Esther, and Tawny were using. She was getting too old to sit on the ground, that was for sure.

"That was Jason Burnes." Tawny sat up and looked over her shoulder too. How had all these women seen him when they were facing the other way? Maybe they were moms.

"Yeah," Lexie said, hoping the conversation would move on. After all, Sasha had promised her they wouldn't talk about men.

"My dad says the papayas are coming on," Esther said. "We can go pick them tomorrow, if you want."

"I'm in," Stacey said. "I'd love to have some for dinner at the Hideaway."

Little conversations similar to that one happened, and Sasha was right. No one brought up the "dreamboat" again —honestly, that was laughable—and they didn't sit and talk about their billionaire husbands.

Lexie found them to be approachable, likable, and enjoyable. She sunned for an hour, and just when she thought she might be burning, she started packing up. "I should go," she said. "I need to call my brother in New York and it's quitting time there."

Winnie had left twenty minutes ago, and Lexie had learned that this was a very loose club. Sasha had told her a bit more about it, and Lexie wondered if she'd passed some sort of initiation.

"Oh, Dreamboat is back," Gina hissed, bending to place something in her bag.

Lexie couldn't help turning to find Jason. Sure enough, he strolled along the beach like he belonged there. As if. He wore the board shorts, sure. But he didn't like the beach, and Lexie knew it.

She refrained from rolling her eyes. Or yelling out to him.

He whistled through his teeth and a dog came tearing over to him.

"Oh, he has a puppy." Gina might as well have clapped her hands and jumped for joy.

A dog? Since when was Jason a dog person? He pointed toward the group of women, and the canine came tearing toward them, a streak in the sand for how fast he could run.

The women squealed, Lexie included, and Jason whistled, stopping the dog on a dime. He sat, his tongue hanging out of his mouth as he grinned at the ladies.

Tawny stomped toward him. "Jason. Don't be a jerk."

"I'm not," he said evenly, almost with a laugh in the back of his throat. "I'm just walking down the beach with my dog."

And without a shirt, as Lexie couldn't seem to stop staring at him. She finally found the brainpower to lift her eyes to his. "You got a dog?"

"Obviously."

"What's his name?" She'd bet a hundred bucks he'd rented the animal just to impress her.

"Steve."

"Steve?" She scoffed. "Who names a dog Steve?"

Jason shrugged. "I adopted him. I don't know who

named him Steve." He bent and scratched the dog's ears. "But it fits him. I couldn't change it."

"What kind of dog is it?" she challenged next. She felt the weight of the other women's eyes on her, and then they moved to Jason.

"He's a Brittany spaniel." Jason looked right into her eyes, and Lexie thought he could see all the inner workings of her soul.

"Did you get him just to impress me?"

Jason tipped his head back and laughed. Laughed and laughed. Humiliation and embarrassment ran through Lexie. Just as she was about to throw her phone at him to get him to stop, he sobered, stepped closer, leaned down.

My, he smelled good. Whatever sunscreen he bought, she wanted to bathe in it. *No, you don't.* She glared at him, their faces only a few inches apart now.

"Believe it or not, Lexie, I got a dog so I wouldn't be so lonely here on the island." He didn't wait for her to respond, and she wouldn't have been able to anyway. The way he'd practically purred her name still had vibrations running through her, making her mind slow and her tongue thick.

He simply whistled again, this time much softer and through puckered lips. "Let's go, Steve. I'm sure we can find someone on this beach who appreciates your name."

With that, he walked past the rest of the women and on down the beach.

FOUR

JASON WALKED with his head held high and his shoulders square, but his ears worked just fine. So he heard, "What was that?" and "Girl, he likes you," and "What's going on with you and Jason Burnes?" coming from the various women behind him.

The infamous Women's Beach Club he'd heard about through the grapevine. And by the grapevine, he meant the hotel lobby, where he'd seen all of those women come in and out together, talking. And that place was made with marble and high ceiling so words carried and echoed.

It wasn't a crime to be observant. To watch. To listen. And Jason was very good at all three of those.

I got a dog so I wouldn't be so lonely here on the island. Lexie was a smart woman. She'd hear the meaning in those words. *I want you, but I can't have you, so Steve'll have to do.* Surely she had some sort of pet too. She'd never liked going home to an empty house, with no one and nothing to greet her.

He turned toward the hotel and the street, glancing casually over to where the women had been. They now walked in a clump, their heads bent together, obviously talking about him. Surprisingly, he didn't mind. Maybe they could convince Lexie he wasn't the monster she thought he was.

Though, judging by the fire in her eyes—borne from anger and desire—she didn't really dislike him. "She dislikes the *idea* of you," he told himself as he walked along the sidewalk to the street. He clipped a leash on Steve then, because the spaniel thought cars wanted to be friends.

He didn't have to work at Sweet Breeze at all today, and most people would be glad for a day off. But not Jason. A day off meant too much time with his own thoughts. He took Steve into the entrance of Getaway Bay, where Sterling worked with another valet that morning. They both greeted him and gave Steve plenty of attention before Jason continued down the beachwalk.

Though it wasn't quite noon yet, the sun beat down on the beach and the line in front of Two Coconuts had already grown to epic proportions. He reached into the large side pocket on his shorts and started handing out drink coupons for The Straw. He'd seen them at Sweet Breeze, and he figured Fisher had an agreement with Sasha to have them there.

"It's just around the bay," he said, talking and answering questions until he ran out of coupons. Several people started walking down the wooden walkway that led through the jungle palms and other trees to the smaller easy bay, where Sasha's stand was.

Jason wasn't sure why he cared if people spent their

money at Two Coconuts or The Straw. Lexie probably wasn't even working today. After all, he'd just seen her at the beach fifteen minutes ago, and she didn't blend at The Straw every day.

Still, his house sat to the east, and he was ready to let Steve off the leash again, so he followed the people he'd just persuaded away from Two Coconuts. He'd never fallen in love with the frozen tropical drinks the way others had, so he took up his usual spot by the palm tree thirty yards from the stand.

Sasha had made it over, but Lexie wasn't anywhere to be found. The Polynesian woman in the window had a bright smile and he'd seen her lots of times in his surveillance of the drink stand.

Steve growled, such an odd behavior that Jason glanced down at the canine. He was lying down, teeth bared as a man passed. He didn't seem any different than anyone else—he wore shorts and an obnoxious floral patterned shirt he'd obviously picked up in the airport. That alone set Jason's alert on high, as it was obvious this man was desperately trying to fit in somewhere he didn't belong.

He joined the line in front of The Straw and ran his hand through his dark hair. He didn't seem tan enough for someone who lived on the island, and that would've tipped Jason off if the hideous shirt hadn't.

Jason just watched as drinks came out the window and the man edged forward. Steve had settled back to sleep in the sand, and Jason's attention wandered. But when the man stepped up to order, the Polynesian woman just looked back at him. She said something Jason obviously couldn't hear and then she called Sasha over to talk to him.

They moved to the side so another order could be taken, and Jason straightened and took a step forward. Steve lumbered to his feet, ready to go. Jason held the leash taut so the dog would stay.

Sasha shook her head and frowned, crossed her arms and seemed determined not to give the man what he wanted. He finally threw up his hands and turned directly toward Jason. The anger wasn't hard to see in the snarl on his face, and he marched through the sand to the more solid boards, striding despite his cheap flip flops.

Jason memorized his face as he came toward him, and the man snapped, "What are you staring at, buddy?" when he went by.

Steve growled again, but Jason held him in place as he watched the man until he disappeared around a curve in the beachwalk. Only then did he look back to The Straw, which seemed to carry on as usual.

His heart started thumping then, his adrenaline kicking in after the situation had resolved. He watched Sasha serve drinks, and when the line died, Jason decided he was really thirsty. He approached the stand, meeting the Polynesian woman's eyes. She wore a name tag that said Maddy, and asked him, "What can I get for you?"

"I've never been here," he said, fully expecting Sasha to turn from the back of the stand and pepper him with questions. She did twist to see who was talking, then she came forward.

"Well, hello, Jason." She spoke in a knowing tone, but Jason had no idea what she knew. "You've never been here?"

"First timer," he declared, bringing out his smile. "I like sour stuff. What do you recommend?" He was sure he wouldn't like any of them, what with names like Berry Blast-off and A Pear of Peaches.

"We've got some lemon and lime concoctions," Sasha said, but Jason shook his head.

"What about mango?" he asked. He liked that, especially the dried stuff with all the sugar on the outside.

"Mango Mountain Majesties is great," Maddy said. "It's peaches and mangoes and orange sherbet."

That did sound absolutely majestic, and he said, "I'll take that."

"Twenty-four or thirty-six?"

"Twenty-four."

"Four sixty-two," Maddy said and Sasha turned to blend his drink into something delicious. He took it from her a few moments later and asked, "What did that man want? The one you were arguing with?"

Her gaze turned cold and hard. "How long have you been standing there watching?"

"Not long."

"Lexie's not coming in today," she said, but she exchanged a glance with Maddy that said otherwise. Jason didn't press the issue, just took a sip of his drink.

"Oh, wow, this is good." He took a longer pull on the straw while Sasha scoffed.

"You thought it wouldn't be?" she asked.

"I wasn't sure," he said. "I've literally never had anything like this."

"Where are you from?" Maddy asked.

"Virginia," he and Sasha said at the same time. He locked eyes with her, pure surprise dancing through him along with the tangy, sweet taste of mangoes and peaches and oranges. And it took a lot to surprise Jason.

"Someone's been talking about me," he said with another smile to mask his true feelings. "What else did Lexie say?" He was sure none of it was good, just like he was sure that man would be back until he got what he was after.

"Nothing," Sasha said, those arms going across her chest again.

"Mm." He drank some more of his smoothie. "Was that other man looking for Lexie?"

Another glance gave Jason his answer, even when Sasha said, "No."

"All right." He jangled the leash and said, "Come on, Steve. Time to go home." He walked in the direction of his house, sipping and thinking and sipping some more. By the time he got home, he'd drank all of the smoothie and come up with the skeleton of a plan.

Find that man and watch him until Jason could figure out who he was, why he was here, and what he wanted with Lexie.

Jason wasn't sure if he was exceptionally skilled at hunting down information or just lucky, but it only took him a few hours to learn that Victor Bunce was a real estate developer out of Jersey City—about as far from Getaway Bay as the man should be.

He was staying at Sweet Breeze, and Jason supposed it was good he had some connections there through Owen Church.

Jason wasn't working security that day, but he had changed out of his swim trunks and into a pair of khakis and a black polo to stand around at the bar like he was waiting for a golfing buddy.

When Victor finally came down from his room around four o'clock, relief flowed through Jason. He wasn't sure how many more sodas he could sip casually. "Thanks, Bert," he said as he set his glass on the counter and threw a fifty dollar bill next to it.

He kept his eyes on the back of Victor's head as he left the hotel, and then Jason turned away from the main exit, pulling his mirrored shades from his pocket when he stepped out of the side door.

Because he was taller and leaner, he had to wait for a moment on the edge of the sidewalk for Victor to show up on the beachwalk. The pudgier man moved with purpose, right back over to the east bay and The Straw.

He didn't get in line this time, and Jason went past him and on down the walkway, taking up a position that showed him Victor's face and body language but not inside the drink stand. He'd already seen that Lexie was indeed working today, and he'd already known she would be.

Sometimes a text was all the espionage he needed to perform.

So Sasha had lied to him. Jason wasn't particularly worried about that. Everyone lied to him. It wasn't personal. But he'd been wondering for hours *why* Sasha had lied to him.

The Straw stayed busy for quite a while, the late afternoon crowd going home merging with the evening crowd just coming to the beach. Jason waited, his attention never staying on Victor for too long, but never quite leaving him either.

Finally, the man got up and approached the stand again, his face already twisted with anger. A moment later, Lexie burst out the side of the drink hut and darted around the back. Every male instinct inside Jason urged him to get across the sand and protect her, but he stayed right where he was.

Sasha came out too, meeting Victor at the door. They spoke, and if it hadn't been so breezy, Jason might have been able to hear some of what they said.

Sasha went around the back of the stand and stood as a barrier between Lexie and Victor, who proceeded to shout at her.

Jason heard that. "It's your fault! We lost everything with your stupid investments. Years wasted. You owe me so much money!" He lunged forward as if he'd grab Lexie and tow her down to the bank right now to get what he thought he was owed.

Sasha stepped in front of him and put her hand on Victor's chest and shoved him back. Lexie fell a few steps in the opposite direction, her face stricken and yet strong. She said something that looked like, "I'm sorry," and something else Jason couldn't lip-read.

Sasha punched a few keys on her phone and lifted it to her ear before Victor held up both hands and backed away. Sasha lowered the phone—obviously her threat to call the police had had the desired effect on Victor—and the two women watched him go back around the stand. Jason watched him too, and he slammed his fist on the metal table where he'd been sitting before continuing down the beachwalk.

Okay, so the man had some suppressed rage. Jason had seen that in men before, and it usually didn't end well for the person on the receiving end of that fury.

And that person was Lexie. He released the fists he'd curled his fingers into and watched as Sasha comforted her. But it really wasn't necessary. Lexie was like iron. She might get a ding or two, but she was strong and could weather almost any storm.

He knew, because he'd watched her do it before. From a distance, just like now. And as Jason stood, half-concealed behind the trees, he vowed he wouldn't be staying in the background this time.

FIVE

LEXIE LEANED against the hut and pushed the loose hair off her forehead as a sigh leaked from her mouth. Coming down off a confrontation always left her weak and exhausted, and she still had hours to go on her shift at The Straw.

"You're okay?" Sasha asked.

"I'm fine." Lexie was about as far from fine as a person could get, but she didn't know what else to say. Victor hadn't touched her, but she felt like the issue with him wasn't over either.

Sasha patted her arm and said, "Take all the time you need," before she rounded the corner and went back inside.

Lexie stayed outside, trying to get her pulse to calm down. She actually had a restraining order against Victor and his company, and she could call it in and get him out of her life. As she settled, all she could think was that Sasha's text could've been a bit more informative.

Lexie had interpreted *There's a man here to see you* as flirtatious and fun, and she'd assumed it had been Jason. And when he'd texted a couple of hours later to find out if she'd be working the stand, she'd readily told him yes.

But she couldn't blame her friend. It wasn't like she'd told Sasha anything about her past. She knew Lexie was rich, but she didn't necessarily know where she'd come from, or how she'd achieved her wealth, or pretty much anything beyond Lexie's ability to do mental math and show up on time.

She drew in a breath for so long she thought she'd burst a lung, then pushed all the air out, out, out. So she'd keep an eye on her back, and she'd make sure Victor didn't cause any more trouble.

She pulled out her phone and called Luke, though it was just after eleven o'clock in New York City. "Hey, Lexie." He didn't sound like he was anywhere near bed.

"What do you know about Victor Bunce and Jersey Shores Realty?"

"Jersey Shores…." Luke took a few seconds to think. "Weren't they one of the companies falsifying the loan documents before the crash?"

That rang a bell in Lexie's mind. "Seems right. And Victor?"

"Let me find out." She heard a slight tapping come through the line. "I'm going to put you on speaker. Tell me what's going on."

Lexie appreciated that Luke knew this wasn't just a casual call. She loved her brothers, but they were usually very business-focused. They didn't have a lot of personal conversations, and she would never call this late at night if it wasn't something important.

"He showed up here on the island," she said. "Waited for me where I work, confronted me, and yelled at me that we owed them money."

"Uh, we don't owe anyone money. All the cases have been resolved."

Lexie sighed again and wiped her forehead with the back of her hand. "I know."

"Let's see. Jersey Shores went out of business when the market collapsed. Bankrupt. Four of their employees went to jail, but Victor wasn't one of them. It doesn't say much about him." His voice echoed slightly, and more clicking sounded in her ear.

She felt like someone was watching her, and she did a quick scan of the beach in front of her, to her right where the sand stretched, and then the left where the bay curved and houses and trees started. Definitely someone over there, and the way it felt like it was a presence with a pull as strong as the sun, it had to be Jason.

He stayed stubbornly out of sight, though she continued to search for him. Had he seen the altercation?

Probably. And the thought did more than embarrass Lexie. She felt helpless, and it had been a long time since she'd felt like that.

"Hey, we have a restraining order against Jersey Shore and Victor Bunce," Luke said.

"Yeah." Lexie didn't know what else to say.

"I'll have our lawyer send it to him again, and remind him it applies to you no matter where you are."

"That would be great," Lexie said. They paid people to take care of problems like this, and Lexie was very glad they did. "Thanks, Luke. That's all. Hey, how did it go with the new investments today?"

"The market is closed until morning. We're going to drop Bangerter then, and get the new investments started first thing."

"You better get to bed then."

Luke chuckled. "Yeah, I better."

Lexie relaxed further once she hung up with her brother, and she went back inside The Straw to find Sasha six orders behind. "I'm so sorry," she said, grabbing a ticket in one hand and a clean blender in another.

Sasha actually stopped working, an action that spoke more than any words ever could've. "Everything okay?" She looked at Lexie—right at her—and Lexie thought she may have a real friend she could trust with anything.

"Yes." She smiled and started scooping strawberries and blackberries into her blender. "Though, next time I have a man come looking for me, maybe clarify that it's not Jason."

Sasha poured a thick, orange liquid into a cup and slapped a lid on it. "You thought it was Jason?"

Lexie shrugged, set the blender on the base and hit the power button before turning to get another ticket.

A few more drinks went out the window before Sasha said, "You guys obviously have a history."

"Yes."

Sasha handed two more cups to customers. "That's all I get? Yes?"

Lexie kept her focus on the recipe she had memorized.

When the last customer of this rush had their refreshment, she leaned against the counter with her back to the beach beyond. "We dated in New York. Well." She shrugged and folded her arms. "It was a big secret, but yeah. He was a bartender at this trendy place downtown, and he was my brother's best friend."

To Sasha's credit, she didn't gasp or squeal or any of the things that would've driven Lexie crazy. "Sounds like that should've worked out."

"The market crashed," Lexie said like that explained everything, but the way Sasha just watched her, waiting for more, said it didn't. "I own an investment firm, right? Well, a lot of our clients had a lot of money in the housing and real estate market. They lost money. We lost money. We were implicated in shady loan practices, and had eight indictments to deal with."

A band of stress settled across her shoulders just saying all that. But she couldn't quit now, even when Sasha said, "Wow."

"Jason lost everything he'd invested. He blamed me, as I'd encouraged him to put his money in real estate. And then, once the media learned about our relationship, he got dragged through some mud too." She hated the way her voice hardly sounded like her own, and all the things she'd tried so hard *not* to think about were suddenly streaming through her mind.

"We broke up when he gave private details about me and Luke, our family and our firm, and I focused on getting things cleaned up at work." She pushed away from the counter as someone approached. The couple ordered and she took their money while Sasha started making the drink.

Once they'd gone, Sasha wiped the counter and said, "Well, I don't think it's over between you two," she said.

"Oh, it is." Lexie focused on restocking all the containers at the back of the stand. That way, when the next rush came, she'd be ready. Hours later, after darkness had fallen and the window had been closed and everything cleaned up for the day, she and Sasha stepped out of the stand. Sasha locked it and turned to her as Jasper stood from where he'd been waiting at one of the tables in front of the hut.

"Do you want us to make sure you get home okay?" Sasha leaned into Jasper, who pressed his lips to her temple, his adoration of her so obvious it make Lexie's jealousy rush to her head.

She'd been looking for a man to come through the line and order a drink—but it wasn't someone like Victor Bunce. Could it be Jason?

She banished the thought as she shook her head. "I'll be fine." She owned a nice home with a security system in a safe neighborhood even if it didn't have a coded gate.

"All right," Sasha said at the same time Jasper said, "What happened?"

Sasha gave him the cliff-notes version as they went up the beach to their cars.

"You sure, Lex?" Jasper watched her, and she appreciated his concern.

"I'm sure."

"Call me when you get home." Sasha gave her a quick hug and ducked into Jasper's sports car.

"Me too," Jasper said.

"Like you won't be with her." Lexie rolled her eyes, though she was happy for her friends.

"Oh, she goes right to bed when we get home." Jasper grinned and chuckled a bit. "I've got a conference call in forty minutes."

"Good luck with it." Lexie gave him a smile and unlocked her car. She drove slowly out of town, only accelerating once she hit the highway. It wasn't horribly late—not like last night when she and Jason had taken their joyride—but there wasn't much traffic either. So it was very easy to see that there was a car following her.

She slowed and turned onto the wrong street, praying she was wrong. That the car would continue past.

It didn't, but turned after her. She immediately yanked the wheel to the left and onto another residential street. There were only four houses down here, and she saw no way to slide into a driveway and quickly shut off her car before the pursuer would see her. And the last thing she needed was to be alone in the middle of the night with Victor Bunce—or anyone for that matter.

So she kept going, the swath of headlights behind her erasing any doubt in her mind that she was being followed. As she turned left again to get back to the highway, another car came into view behind the first.

Great. Two stalkers. Just what she needed. She kept her left blinker on, because she couldn't lead them to her home. Her phone rang while she waited for the other two cars to catch up to her or pull over and basically announce that they were following her.

Exasperation added to the fear and frustration tumbling through her. "What, Jason?"

"I'm in the second car back," he said in a no-nonsense voice she imagined he'd perfected during his time as a police officer and a private detective. "My place or yours?"

"Mine," Lexie said without thinking. Though it was dark, she sat under a street light. When she looked in her rear-view mirror and managed to meet the eyes of Victor Bunce, she held up her finger and wagged it like he'd be in trouble if he continued to follow her.

So she turned right, relieved when he turned left. Practically sagging in her seat, she drove slowly along the highway, Jason now right behind her.

She led him to her house, suddenly self-conscious about letting him into her space. She took great pride in her yard and the interior design of her place, and Jason, with his all-seeing eyes, would dress it down within a moment, make judgments, and then say the place looked like her.

She pulled into the garage and left it open for him to park beside her. Once he was in, she closed it again before getting out of her car at the same time he did. Their eyes met, and Lexie had a flashback to the last time they'd stood in a small space together like this.

He'd said, "I have to talk to them, Lex. They won't leave me alone, and I have nowhere to hide."

"Then talk to them," she'd said. She couldn't imagine him as anything but the sexy, handsome man she'd fallen in love with. The loyal, hardworking bartender who would never betray her—until he did.

I didn't leak that story. His words from last night, when he'd approached her in front of Fisher's private elevator. As she heard them in her mind now, they had a ring of truth to them. She hadn't told Luke about Jason's appearance on the island, and she wondered what he could dig up on his once-best friend.

"Are we going to go in?" he asked. "Or stand in the garage."

Lexie flew into motion, striding around the front of her car and up the few steps to the entrance to the house. She couldn't remember if she'd left her breakfast dishes in the sink or not, or what the guest bathroom looked like. She frantically scanned the entry way and found it mostly clean, with a pair of shoes by the decorative table there.

She swept them into her hands before Jason could see. She went around the steps leading to the second floor and threw the shoes in the little room concealed behind them, pulling the door closed just as he came in the house.

"Wow, Lex, this place is nice." Sure enough, he scanned everything from the high ceilings to the paint color to the table where she had all of her fondest photos. He stepped over to that and examined the framed pictures of her and her brothers, her family, and one with her and the Nine-0 Club, which she'd taken when they'd come to the house last summer for one of their meetings.

She turned away from him so she wouldn't have to watch him look extra-hard at that picture or answer any questions he might have about it. Along with the photos, Lexie had little mementos from Getaway Bay that she'd collected in the five years she'd been living here. They'd all been tastefully chosen and color-coordinated with the photos. Not that Jason needed to know that.

In the kitchen, she started making coffee, her go-to drink whenever she needed to relax. Strange, what with the caffeine, but if she added enough cream and sugar, it was almost like drinking hot milk before bed.

"Coffee?" she asked as Jason joined her.

"You pick out this furniture yourself?"

Why he was asking, she had no idea. "Yes." She didn't mean to clip the word out, but he was literally the only person on the planet she'd told about her dreams of being an interior designer. But she was a Keller, of Keller Investments, and one didn't just walk away from that.

"Black," he said, the two conversations they were having getting criss-crossed. Lexie could follow it fine though, and she set out the sugar bowl and got the container of cream from the fridge.

"You've always wanted silver tiles in your kitchen." He spoke with a fondness in his voice that Lexie had heard on previous occasions, usually just before he kissed her. Everything was spiraling out of control, and she moved out of the kitchen where he stood admiring her backsplash.

She *had* always wanted silver tiles, another fact she'd shared with only him. Maybe Sasha was right when she'd said what she'd had with Jason wasn't over.

Has to be, she told herself. She'd made a clean break from that life, and she wasn't going back.

But it didn't seem like Jason wanted to go back either. And the clear line Lexie had drawn between her old self and her new one had started to blur considerably.

"So," he said as the coffee started percolating. "What are we going to do about Victor?"

"I have a restraining order against him." Lexie walked into the living room and collapsed on her soft leather couch with a long sigh. "Luke is having the lawyers send a reminder."

"You think that will be enough?" Jason came into the living room too, his tall body and broad shoulders filling the whole house with his powerful presence. His charisma had been the first thing that had drawn Lexie to him at the bar. And it still called to her now.

"I don't know. He didn't follow me here."

Jason gave her a calculated look and sat down beside her. "Lex, he sure did."

"What?" Alarm sang through her.

"He was a ways back," Jason said. "I'm not sure if he knows which house is yours. But he didn't go back to the hotel."

"How do you know it was him?"

"Intuition."

And Jason had a lot of that, and Lexie had learned not to ignore it. That same sense of helplessness filled her and her face tightened and her emotions rolled through her, choking her, making her eyes hot with tears.

"Hey, come on." Jason put his arm around her and pulled her against his side. "We don't cry over scumbags like Victor Bunce."

"Yes, we do," Lexie said.

"The Lexie Keller I knew didn't."

"I'm a different Lexie Keller now." She sat up out of his

embrace, immediately missing the warmth of his body and the comfort of his vibrating voice moving through her.

"Not that different," he said, looking at her with something peculiar in his eyes. She couldn't quite name it before he wiped it away.

"So what do you want to do? Stalk me too?"

He ducked his head, half a smile touching his mouth. Lexie remembered when she'd kissed that mouth, and wow, seven years was not long enough to dull some memories.

"I was thinking maybe…." He lifted his eyes to hers. "We pretend. You know, me and you. I'm your boyfriend. I'm jealous. Victor better back off."

Lexie stared, blinked, and then burst out laughing. She stood up, needing a mega-huge cup of coffee right now. "Yeah, I don't think so." She got down two mugs and though the coffee wasn't quite finished yet, she paused the machine and poured two cup's worth.

"Do you have a better idea?" He joined her in the kitchen, taking a seat at the bar and facing her as she slid his mug toward him.

"Anything's better than that." Because she knew, with Jason Burnes, there was no pretending. The man did things one hundred percent, or he didn't do them at all.

"I'm all ears." He lifted his mug to his lips and sipped. Lexie had never been jealous of a coffee mug before, but she was now. Just by having him in her home for this conversation would infuse the air with the delectable scent of his cologne for days.

Lexie stirred sugar and cream into her coffee, every cell in her body begging her to take them to bed. She didn't have to work at The Straw tomorrow, and maybe they could talk about this then.

She didn't have to work....

"How often do you valet at Sweet Breeze?" she asked.

"A few nights a week."

"And your security gig?"

"Whenever Owen schedules me."

She could see his mind whirring, trying to catch onto what she was getting at. "I know Owen," she said. "I'll talk to him."

Jason set his mug down and folded his arms in front of him on the counter. The urge to lunge across the island and kiss him drove Lexie toward the brink of insanity. She was too tired to be around him. Too emotional. The last time she'd felt like this, they'd ended up in Jason's office, the door locked, while she kissed him and kissed him and kissed him.

"Talk to him about what?" Jason asked, even the sound of his voice throaty and beautiful.

"Hiring you to be my bodyguard," she said.

SIX

JASON STARED AT LEXIE. "I'm sorry. Bodyguard?"

"Not to be confused with boyfriend," she said, taking a swig of her coffee. Surely it was too hot for that, but with the amount of cream she'd stirred in, maybe not. He'd worked hard not to make a face when she'd ruined perfectly good coffee. She'd always liked it to taste less like coffee than anything else, and he'd teased her about it enough for one lifetime.

"The two B-words shouldn't be confused," she said. "Got it?"

Jason could barely keep up with the conversation. "I don't think I've got anything."

"Let's be clear, then." She glared at him with those gorgeous eyes, and he wanted to kiss her so, so badly. For a moment there, on the couch, he thought she'd melt a little, let him hold her like he used to, let him back into her life, her heart. Even just getting through the door of her home was impressive.

"I need a bodyguard," she said. "You don't really have a job. You're big. You're strong. You can look scary. I'll pay you to watch me. You're doing it for free now. This is a step up."

"I don't watch you twenty-four-seven," he shot back. "Being a bodyguard is totally different than what I've been doing."

"But you've been doing something."

Of course he had. She knew that. He didn't need to say it out loud, though she seemed to be probing for just that.

"So you want me to move in here?"

"I…hadn't thought that far ahead." The trepidation on her face said she didn't want him here. But somewhere, deep down inside her, she probably did. Jason had seen this kind of indecision before—when her father had met with her, needing to know if he should put her in the will as the owner and operator of the company. His cirrhosis of the liver had advanced, and she'd been as distraught over his health as much as she hadn't been sure if she should take over the investment firm. Jason had simply held her while they talked it all through, knowing she would in the end. And she had.

And he could also predict how this situation would end, and he wondered if he'd even kept the ratty luggage he'd come to Hawaii with—because when things went south, he'd be forced to leave again.

"This place seems pretty big," he said lightly, as if he didn't care one way or the other. But the pumping of his blood through his veins said differently. He really liked

Lexie Keller, and he always had, and if she needed him, he wanted to be right there beside her.

You'll have to tell her what really happened in New York.

For the first time, the thought didn't have Jason running for the exit. Maybe it was time to get everything out in the open. Time to heal those wounds. Time to move forward. Time to see if any of the love they'd once had could be rekindled.

For him, some of it already had been, and the private detective in him knew she felt the same about him.

"Want to give me a tour?" he asked, standing and leaving his half-empty mug on the counter.

"Fine." She had some snap to her voice, but it didn't bother Jason. He'd seen Lexie Keller angry, and this wasn't it. Plus, he wanted to follow her around and discover anything he'd missed in the past seven years. He'd missed her more than he knew, and he'd acknowledged that after they'd broken up, he'd experienced the lowest point of his life.

Everything in her house was beautiful and straight, just like her. He wanted to grab onto one of the gray, gauzy curtains in the guest bathroom and ruffle it up a little bit. He kept his hands to himself instead.

She led him around a house that looked exactly like it fit her, and the atmosphere felt comfortable and lived in, despite her extreme attention to detail and order. She talked about her choices of colors for each room, and how they'd spoken to her as she designed the house. With a private office beside her bedroom and a huge living room, her main floor could've easily accommodated four of his houses.

And upstairs was even more impressive. As she led him into a comfortable loft, he imagined himself lounging there, something on the TV while he talked to Lexie about her day, strategized for how to keep her safe, and kissed her before he went down the hall to one of the three bedrooms.

"I could stay in this one," he said, being very careful not to use the word "live." He did not want to suggest they live together. But if she was serious about this bodyguard thing—and Jason believed she was—he wouldn't be able to stay in his beach bungalow and be here to protect her.

"This one would work for you," she said as equally as careful. "It's the biggest one, and I don't ever come up here." She stood in the doorway with him, looking around the room as if she could imagine him there.

They'd dated secretly for a year, and since they couldn't even really be seen in public together, the idea of them living together had never come up. Lexie was traditional in that regard, anyway, as the biggest reason for their secret rendezvous were because she'd always dreamt of having her father walk her down the aisle, and her father would definitely not have approved of his daughter—the heiress of a multi-billion dollar investment firm—marrying someone like Jason.

But the man had died six years ago, a year after the catastrophic events that had torn Lexie from him. She'd been engaged to another man by then, but she still hadn't gotten that picture-perfect wedding she'd dreamed about.

Thinking of that made Jason's heart ache for her, and he wondered what she was thinking. So he asked her.

"I don't know," she said, her voice almost childlike.

"You don't know what you're thinking about?"

She gazed up at him, more vulnerable than he'd seen her since moving to the island. "What are you thinking about?"

"When we were together," he said simply, honestly. "About how you wanted your father to walk you down the aisle at your wedding." A smile touched his lips, and it felt like a really long time since his lips had curved that way.

His fingers drifted across hers, and he latched on, taking a moment to settle his in the spaces between hers.

"I was thinking that you hate gray paint, and this whole room is gray."

He glanced around it again and said, "I don't hate it."

"But you don't like it."

"Would you let me paint it?"

She hesitated, and Jason squeezed her hand. "Lex, you haven't changed as much as you think you have."

She drew in a breath and turned to go into the hall. He released her fingers, wishing he could simply latch on again, but walking down the hall they couldn't exactly be side-by-side, and it felt awkward. She poked her head into the other two rooms, but she was right. That one right off the lounge was perfect, and he'd definitely move into that one if she was serious about hiring him.

"There's a basement too," she said when they landed back on the main level. "But I use it for storage mostly."

Jason hated that she seemed right back to her impersonal persona, and he wanted to go back upstairs and make the real Lexie come back.

"How do you feel about dogs?" he asked. "I mean, if you're serious about this. *Are* you serious about this?"

Lexie hugged herself as if cold, and she did keep the house pretty chilly. "I think I need to be. Name your salary."

Jason would work for free if he could spend his time with Lexie, but he couldn't say that. So he said, "Whatever you think is fair," and swiped his keys from where he'd left them on the kitchen counter. He hesitated, looked her in the eye, and said, "Am I starting tonight?"

Fear paraded through her expression, and Jason put his keys down. "All right." He wasn't sure if he should be happy with this new arrangement or not. "And you said you'd talk to Owen? I'll need my job back after this is done."

"I'll call him right now." She pulled her phone from her pocket and wandered away from Jason. "Hey, Owen," she said, shooting a look over her shoulder. Jason supposed she did have an in with the man if she could call him this late at night and get him to pick up on the first ring.

Jason moved over to the double doors off the dining area that led outside, wanting to give Lexie more privacy. But when he glanced behind him, she'd disappeared. So he opened the doors and went out onto a deck that spanned to the right and left and overlooked the yard. The darkness here reigned supreme, and he wondered if she'd done her house hunting in the dead of night.

He looked up into the sky, finding the stars easily and grinning at them. "Please," he said, but he'd never been much for religion and church, and he had no idea how to finish. He settled on the top step of the stairs and rested his elbows on his knees.

She joined him a few minutes later, sitting beside him as she said, "It's done. You'll just keep your valet job. Owen said he couldn't let you go from that. I guess they're desperate."

"Yeah, Sterling's been having some family problems and couldn't work overnight anymore."

"Oh."

Jason lifted his arm and Lexie snuggled into him, and in that moment—that single moment—he tasted happiness again. It had been a while, and there was no one he wanted to share it with more than the woman beside him.

"You'll be okay overnight while I'm at Sweet Breeze?" he asked.

"I should be," she said. "It's more about the appearance of you, anyway. So you'll have to stop strutting around the beach in your swimwear. I want a suit, Mister, and I want it to be pressed and straight."

Jason tipped his head toward those stars she loved and laughed. "Yes, ma'am."

"Do you own a suit?" she asked.

"I used to have a real job," he said. "I have a couple of suits." Not ones he'd consider high-end to be a billionaire's bodyguard, though.

"We'll go shopping in the morning," she said, eliciting a groan from Jason. She nudged him with her shoulder and said, "Come on. I've never had a bodyguard, and I want you to look like the freaking Secret Service."

He looked down at her, and the light from the moon fell across her face in such a way that she appeared to be glowing. Radiant. His angel.

"You had a bodyguard for a few weeks right after the story broke," he said. As soon as the words left his mouth, he wanted to take them back. But he couldn't. And he wanted her to know he knew. "He became your fiancé if I remember right."

Lexie's face blanched and she squirmed out from underneath his arm. She stood, brushed off her shorts, and said, "We all make mistakes, Jason," before going inside.

Her words branded him, making his skin sear and his jaw clench. But what was he going to do? Go barging into her bedroom and yell at his boss—and the woman he wanted to be his? What would that accomplish?

Nothing.

So he sat on the back steps until his anger had simmered down, and then the went inside, locking the sliding door behind him and going up to his new bedroom. He could sleep in the buff as well as the next man, and tomorrow, he'd bring over everything he needed to be comfortable—including Steve, whom Lexie had never commented on but better get used to. Because Jason had a feeling he wasn't going to be any less lonely in this house than he was in his small cottage on the beach.

SEVEN

LEXIE LAY IN BED, the echo of Jason's hand still burning against her palm and between her fingers. It had felt so nice to hold hands with a man again, as it had been a very long time for Lexie. She'd had few relationships here on the island. To be honest, she hadn't really tried more than a couple of times, and they had both been worthless.

She realized she'd never called or texted Sasha or Jasper, so she sent quick messages to both of them. Only Jasper answered, and he said he'd tell his wife, who had already fallen asleep.

Lexie wanted to wander out to the kitchen and dig through the cupboards until she found a forgotten box of cookies. But she had no idea where Jason was, and she didn't want to face him right now.

We all make mistakes.

What a cruel thing to say. She shouldn't have said it, and she'd known it the moment it had popped into her mind.

She'd allowed it to come out of her mouth anyway, and regret lanced through her like a hot knife.

And yes, she'd had a bodyguard before, and no he hadn't become her fiancé. It was a touch satisfying to know that Jason could be wrong, but seeing as how Lexie had fallen for her temporary bodyguard's *boss*, it wasn't much better.

Derrick Lancaster was everything her father wanted for her, and Lexie could admit that was half the reason she'd been interested in him in the first place. After that, he turned out to be charming—if there were people and cameras around. He could be generous, if there was someone watching. And he could act loving, if the situation required it.

But behind closed doors, the man who would take over the huge Lancaster television empire one day was cold, distant, and ruthless. She'd been thankful every day since their breakup that she'd found him cheating on her with a nightly news anchor. She couldn't even remember feeling sad, or hurt. Just relieved.

She'd been in so far that she wore a diamond ring on her finger. Neither of them wanted to pick a date, but they carried on to the public as if they were blissfully happy and just searching for the right time.

Whatever Jason had seen in the tabloids and on TV wasn't real. She wanted to tell him that, confess that every time she kissed Derrick she imagined it was Jason. Her phone buzzed on the nightstand, and she snatched it up, hoping it was Jason and she could issue a written apology.

But it was Sasha who'd said, *Thanks for letting me know. How are things with Jason?*

How did she know Jason had followed her home? As far as Lexie knew, the two didn't have any connection.

So Lexie said *Jason?* and sent the text.

Several seconds passed where Lexie obsessed over Jason. She'd lived like this for weeks after their break-up too, and it didn't feel pleasant to be returning to the past.

He texted Tyler to go get Steve. So Tawny texted me to see what I knew, and I didn't know anything, but I figured maybe you guys… ???

Lexie was still trying to find something to tell her when another message came in. *I mean, I know you said there was nothing between you, but I can sort of feel the flame myself whenever you're together.*

You've been with us once.

He came and asked about you today. It's obvious he still likes you. Really likes you.

Lexie shook her head and typed out: *I was cruel to him tonight.*

Then apologize. Sasha made it sound so simple, but she didn't know Jason the way Lexie did.

Lexie sat up straighter. She didn't know Jason the way Lexie did.

She jumped out of bed and practically ran to her bedroom door. She paused, listening to hear if anyone moved out in the hallway. But he would've had to be practically standing right outside the door, or banging pots and pans around in the kitchen, for her to hear him.

She'd need to be brave if she was going to pull off this apology, so she pulled open the door and stepped into the hall. Jason was nowhere to be found. The sliding door off the dining room was closed and locked, and she cast a glance up the stairs before moving past them and going into the kitchen.

She knew Jason better than anyone else, and she knew two things about him. One, he adored chocolate chip cookies. And two, he didn't sleep much. So she creamed butter and sugar, dropped in eggs, measured flour, and dumped in a whole bag of milk chocolate chips as quickly and quietly as she could.

Twelve minutes later, she pulled the first sheet tray out of the oven. Instead of setting it on the stovetop, she took it to the bottom of the stairs and waved the aroma upward as if that would do the trick and get him to come down.

Another twelve minutes passed, and another batch of cookies came out of the oven. Lexie deemed twenty-four cookies enough for two people and turned off the oven. Leaving the leftover cookie dough—another delicacy according to Jason—on the counter, she piled six cookies on a plate and poured a tall glass of milk.

If he wouldn't come downstairs, she'd go up.

Sixty seconds later, her heart beat wildly in her chest, and not just from her march up the seventeen steps. She really needed to get going on an exercise routine. She took a deep breath and balanced the plate of cookies on the forearm of the hand holding the milk. With her now-free hand, she banged on the door.

But the motion was too much for the plate, and gravity tipped it toward the outside of her arm. Everything happened so fast, and she wasn't sure exactly which order things went down. No matter what, all the cookies landed on the floor. Milk splashed her hand. And Jason opened the door.

He wore only his pants, a fact that almost sent Lexie to her knees too. "Do you know what time it is?" he asked, his voice in the lower register, as if he'd actually been asleep.

She scrambled to pick up the cookies—and keep her eyes off his naked upper half. "I baked you cookies," she said, standing and presenting him with the treat.

"Those have been on the floor." He chin-nodded to the cookies like they were now infested with maggots.

"Ten second rule."

"It's almost midnight." So he was going to play it the hard way.

"You don't sleep," she shot back.

"Well, I don't eat sugar at midnight." He clenched his jaw as if trying to keep the saliva inside.

And with a torso and chest like the one in front of her, she believed him. The fight went out of her. "I wanted to say…I needed to apologize. What I said to you on the deck was mean. I shouldn't have said it." She picked up a cookie and took a bite without removing her gaze from him. "Mm."

His whole body sighed, and he said, "Let me put on my shirt," before dropping back into the shadowy recesses of his room. A few seconds later, he came all the way into the hall, pulling the door closed behind him as if he had a room full of personal items he didn't want her to see.

"You baked these?"

"My grandmother's recipe." They moved into the loft, and Jason sank into the sofa with a soft groan. Lexie settled next to him, facing him, her knees tucked under her body, and offered him the cookies. He took one from the plate and dusted it off as if her carpet was full of lint.

Lexie rolled her eyes. "Do you accept my apology?"

"I haven't even had one bite yet." His eyes—dark and dreamy and dangerous—locked onto hers and he lifted the cookie to his lips. He took a bite and let his eyes drift closed as if in bliss. He chewed and nodded. After swallowing, he said, "Apology accepted."

He finished the cookie and ate another before he ran his hands through his hair, making it stand up a little on the top.

"You were wrong, you know," Lexie said, wanting to be with him just a little longer.

"I'm sure you'll tell me all about it." His words could've cut, but he delivered them with a flirtatious smirk that kept the sting from settling in too deep.

"My bodyguard wasn't my fiancé."

Interest lit up his face. "Oh?"

"He was a temporary bodyguard until I could find my own. He really worked for Derrick Lancaster, and *he's* who I started dating."

"And got engaged to." He folded his arms. "Six months after we'd broken up." Hurt flashed across his face, and while Lexie didn't like it, the emotion did testify to her that Jason was human. Jason had feelings. Perhaps Jason hadn't gotten over her very quickly, the way she hadn't gotten over him for months and months.

She didn't want to tell him that her new relationship and association with a very wealthy, New York City family, had helped the story of her torrid love affair with the bartender go away faster. Jason had never been a problem for Lexie.

"My dad…." She let the words hang there, because Jason would get them.

"Yeah." He leaned his head back against the couch and closed his eyes. "Family relationships are tough."

Lexie leaned her elbow in to the back of the couch and rested her head in her hands. "Do you talk to your brothers?"

He shook his head, his lips pressing tight for a moment. "Not often."

She wanted to reach out and brush that lock of hair off his forehead, trace her fingertips along his earlobe. Such intimate gestures offered support, comfort, and he needed it right now. So she extended her hand, and lightly touched his hair, causing his eyes to fly open. As she ran her fingers over his ear, he turned his head toward her, and their eyes locked.

"Sorry about your brothers," she said.

"It's time for me to be a real adult," he said, the awkwardness between them gone. "I know that. I just don't know what I want to do with my life."

"I'm guessing it's not valeting."

"Sterling seems to have made a living doing it." Jason looked away, his eyes settling somewhere else in the loft. "I don't know. I feel like I'm…drifting, and I don't know where I'll end up."

She traced her fingers down his bicep and he uncrossed his arms so he could receive her hand. "You've always been a drifter, Jason. It's part of your charm." She gave him a small smile when he looked at her again.

"I have charm?"

"Loads of it." She twisted so her feet were off the front of the couch and snuggled into his side. A few minutes passed while she thought through the events of the past couple of days. Jason's breathing evened and slowed, but Lexie asked, "Do you really think Victor is violent?" anyway.

"I don't know, sweetheart." He squeezed her fingers. "Better safe than sorry, right?"

Sweetheart.

Lexie basked in the sunshine streaming from the word. She closed her eyes too, her fantasies about opening a closed door and letting Jason back into her life playing in full color. The next time she opened her eyes, the sun was just starting to light another day, and Jason still slept beside her.

Lexie took the opportunity to absorb the handsomeness of his face without any tension or emotion in it. He looked peaceful and beautiful, and she focused on his mouth. She'd kissed that mouth when he was awake, and she'd kissed him awake too. Could she do it again?

She hadn't moved. Well, maybe her eyelids. So when Jason said, "I can feel you staring at me," she broke into laughter and lightly swatted at his chest. He cracked one eyelid and smiled as he flinched from her touch.

"I was going to kiss you," she said. "And you ruined it."

That got him to open his eyes, but Lexie was already pushing herself off the couch. He grabbed her hand so she couldn't leave. "Is that part of the job? Kissing?"

She leaned forward, encouraged and a bit scared by the hopeful glint in his eye. "Definitely not," she said. "Don't confuse your B-words, Mister Burnes." She moved away from him, and he let her hand go. "And get up and get ready. We've got to go buy you a couple of suits today. Nice ones."

He groaned but he stood up too. "They won't even be open until at least ten."

"Great." She flashed him a smile before starting down the steps and calling back, "You have time to make me breakfast. That *is* part of the job."

He said something, but she didn't catch what because her giggles had returned in full force.

EIGHT

JASON FIDDLED with the buttons on the jacket, not understanding how this suit was any different than the previous three he'd put on. He was beginning to think Lexie and the three—yes, three—saleswomen waiting outside the dressing room were simply enjoying the fashion show.

Sure enough, when he opened the door and exited the fitting area, he found all four women sitting on the chairs there. If they had popcorn, it would be a real show.

"Turn," Lexie commanded, and Jason glared at her before complying. Women must not know how keen a man's hearing was, because he could plainly make out, "Yeah, that's nice across the shoulders," and "Too bad he's wearing that jacket at all."

Jason looked over his shoulder and said, "I can hear you."

Two of the saleswomen jumped up, and one waggled her

fingers at Jason like he'd be interested in getting her number later.

Lexie got up too and approached, pulling on his sleeves and brushing her hands down the front of the jacket. He held very still, trying to figure out how he'd gotten to this point in his life. How he'd gone from watching Lexie from a thirty-yard distance to holding her hand and sleeping over at her house.

"I like this one," she said.

"Hallelujah." He used no inflection in his voice. They'd been shopping for almost two hours, and he'd lost patience after ten minutes. "Can we go to lunch now?"

Yes, he'd made breakfast, but it was scrambled eggs and toast, five hours ago, and while he didn't sleep much—except for last night. Last night, he'd fallen asleep with Lexie and stayed asleep all night long—he did eat. Never skipped meals. And his stomach growled to prove it.

"Yes, we can go to lunch now, you big baby." She grinned up at him, and it seemed natural for her to tip up on her toes and meet his mouth with hers. The moment lengthened, and neither of them moved.

"So this one and the black one?" The remaining saleswoman broke the connection between them, and Jason fell back a step, clearing his throat as he did.

"Yes," Lexie said. "My card is on file."

"I can buy the suits," he said.

"Nope." Lexie nodded at the saleswoman and waited for her to walk away. "You wouldn't need them if not for me. I'm paying." She gave him a look that dared him to argue.

"Fine." He returned to the dressing room to put on his

own clothes, not wanting to argue over trivial things. With Lexie, there were some hills worth dying on. Her buying him two suits so he could be her bodyguard wasn't one of them.

Lunch, however, was.

He pulled on his shirt and adjusted the hem as he walked out, patting his back pocket to make sure he still had his wallet. Just because Lexie was loaded didn't mean she was going to pay for his food. In fact, *he'd* like to pay for hers, make this more of a date than an employee thing.

But she wasn't standing where he'd left her. Nor at the register. Panic started to build in his stomach, but he kept it dormant as he scanned the department store. The woman who'd been helping them stood behind the counter, and he approached her. "Hey, did you see where the woman I was with went?"

"Someone came over and started talking to her. I didn't see where they went." She indicated his suit. "Do you want this? I'll get the other one wrapped for you."

"Can you hold them for a minute?" He turned without waiting for her to answer. He yanked his phone out of his pocket and dialed Lexie, muttering, "Come on, Lex. Pick up."

She didn't pick up, and as the call went to voicemail, Jason jogged out from between the racks of clothes that were seriously hindering his eyesight. His mind ran in a thousand directions, to how long he'd been in the dressing room changing, to if he'd heard her call for help, to praying to know which way to go.

To his left was the shoe department—and no way out. If

someone had taken her, they wouldn't go that way, at least if they were smart at all. So he turned right and ran down the aisle, scanning, looking, searching for Lexie's dark hair and bright purple blouse.

Thankful he'd paid attention to her wardrobe that morning, he caught a flash of the bright color near the wide entrance to the store. He dashed that way, realizing it was Lexie and she was speaking to another woman. Not Victor. Didn't look threatening.

He slowed and covered the last few feet at a walk, interrupting the conversation by stepping directly to Lexie's side and whispering, "You couldn't have texted me?"

She glanced up into his face, surprise on hers, which melted into realization and then sorrow. "Oh, Jason, I'm so sorry." She looked at the other woman, another brunette, and Jason looked at her too. She looked somewhat familiar, and he knew he'd probably parked her car a time or two at Sweet Breeze. Jason might not remember every name he encountered, but he never forgot a face.

"This is Gabi Rossi. She's an old friend."

"An old friend?" Jason took a protective half-step in front of Lexie and scanned the vast expanse of mall he could see as if expecting an attack at any moment.

Gabi simply blinked at him, and Jason realized he was acting like a bulldog not a bodyguard. Lexie knew it too, because she put her hand on Jason's arm and nudged him back again.

"I've had a bit of trouble," she explained to Gabi, making her voice light and airy and so false Jason was sure her friend wouldn't buy a single thing Lexie said. "Jason's my new bodyguard, and well, as you can see, he's a bit enthusiastic."

Enthusiastic? She'd left the area where they were without telling him, and she hadn't picked up her phone when he called. But he ground his teeth together and said nothing. Bodyguards were supposed to blend in, be overlooked, go unnoticed.

So he moved back, wishing he was wearing one of those fancy suits right now so he looked the part a little better. He stayed out of the way until they finished talking, then she returned to him and they went back to the register in silence. He accepted the suits from the clerk, and when they finally exited the mall to sunshine and an almost-summer breeze, she said, "I'm sorry, Jason."

It was the third time she'd apologized to him in the last twenty-four hours, and he forgave her instantly. "All you had to do was text."

"I didn't even think of it."

He opened the back door of her car and hung his suits on the hook above the window. "Gotta start thinking about it, sweetheart. I'm not just arm candy." He held out his hand for the keys, and her eyebrows went up.

"What do you think you're doing?"

"I'm *starving*," he said. "So I'm taking us to lunch, and I want it to be a surprise."

Lexie didn't like surprises. Sure, she'd allowed them in the past, but usually only on her birthday or another *super* special occasion. Which lunch was not. She didn't make a move to dig in her purse to find her keys and pass them over to him.

"Come on, Lexie. If we stand here much longer, I'm going to start gnawing on your arm."

"My chicken arms?" She gave him a coy smile.

"I only said that once," he said. "And you *do* have skinny arms. It's a fact."

"Sometimes facts don't need to be stated explicitly, especially when it's your girlfriend, and she's already self-conscious about her arms." She cocked her head as if to say *So there.*

All he could hear was *girlfriend*. Endlessly, it reverberated inside his head, even when her mouth moved and she said something else. Only when she slapped the sharp, metal keys into his palm did he snap out of the trance.

"Fine," she said. "But just because I live in Hawaii doesn't mean I want to eat seafood all the time." She marched around the front of the car and practically ripped the door off its hinges.

Jason leaned against his door, facing her. "And no red meat, right? You're still doing that?"

"*That* is a normal thing," she said.

Jason disagreed, but he didn't feel like the time was right to argue his point.

"Are you going to get in?" she asked. "I don't want to roast in there."

He opened his door with a grin and got behind the wheel, started the car, and turned the air conditioning up all the way just as Lexie straightened her shorts and buckled her seat belt. "I'd like somewhere with a great Cobb salad," she said. "Please."

"Which is exactly why I'm driving."

"Jason." He loved the hint of whine in her voice, loved hearing his name come out of her mouth, and loved that he'd somehow wiggled his way back into her life. Now he just needed to figure out how to keep her there.

Ten minutes later, he pulled to a stop in front of a little bistro that had just opened up six weeks ago. He felt sure Lexie wouldn't have been here yet, and he'd actually seen a Cobb salad on their menu. He also happened to like the angus sliders and the shrimp pasta primavera, so he was already chalking this lunch up to be a win.

"Bora's?" Lexie leaned forward to read the sign. "What is this place?"

"Come try it," he said. "It's great."

"You've eaten here?"

He didn't want to tell her that he'd been sampling a lot of places on the island since he'd decided to stay. He had money from his previous job, and he'd become friends with Tyler, who didn't have a job at all. While his wife taught beach yoga, sometimes Tyler and Jason went to lunch. It wasn't a crime.

"Yes," he said simply. "And they have a Cobb salad."

That got her out of the car, and Jason held the door open for her so she could enter the bistro first. It wasn't busy—it never was—and they sat and ordered within a couple of minutes.

He reached across the table and took her hands in his, feeling brave but also out of sorts. "I think I need more rules," he said, rubbing his thumb across the back of her hand.

"Oh, yeah? About what?"

"About…us. Like, am I on duty right now? Can't hold your hand? Can't, oh, I don't know, kiss you after our lunch date?" He watched her, needing to see her reaction so he could judge how fast or slow he needed to go.

"I don't know, Jason." She gently pulled her hands back and unwrapped a straw.

"What don't you know?" Because there were a few obvious things to him.

She pointed to him and then her and then put the straw in her water glass.

"I like you," he said. "I've never stopped liking you, and I know you probably need answers about what happened." He swallowed, not quite sure he was ready to talk about everything yet. He amended the thought. Of course he was. He wanted Lexie in his life, and he would tell her the truth. She deserved that much whether they were going to be together or not.

Lexie looked at him, and dropped her eyes to the table again. "It took me a very long time to get over you," she said, her voice barely carrying across the tiny table between them.

"I never got over you," he said.

She lifted her gaze to him again. "Yeah?"

"Nope. Never did." He hadn't tried all that hard, either. While Jason might not have any idea what to do with his life, he did know who he wanted to figure it out with.

"We have to go slow," she said. "Let me think about things."

"Lex." He waited while the waiter served them their food. Once she was gone, Jason continued. "You've always set the pace in our relationship. It won't be any different this time."

She nodded and picked up her fork. "This does look great."

"It's a salad." He rolled his eyes. "Can't be that great."

"Hey." She picked up a piece of tomato and launched it at him. It flew right over his head and landed on another table. She giggled and covered her mouth with her hand while Jason checked to see if anyone had witnessed the flying fruit.

"Okay, you're a really bad aim," he said, reaching for his first slider.

"Mm," she said, drawing the sound out. "This salad is *so* good."

Later that afternoon, Jason stood in his bedroom/living room, sorting through his clothes. Lexie had gone into the backyard, which was really just a big sand box, to make a phone call. Tyler was supposed to be stopping by at any time to return Steve, and Jason still hadn't packed anything for the dog to come with him to Lexie's house.

He couldn't believe he'd told her he'd never gotten over her. "But it's the truth," he muttered to himself, looking at a pair of shorts he wasn't sure were clean or not. And he was committed to telling her the truth. After all, he now knew the consequences if he didn't, and he couldn't watch her walk out of his life again.

The front door opened and Tyler said, "Hey," as Steve's

paws clickety-clacked against the hard floor. He ran right over to Jason, who dropped the shorts in favor of scrubbing down his dog. Lazy Bones, Tyler's golden retriever, followed, a happy smile on his face.

"Hey, Stevie," he said. "Were you good for Tyler? Yeah? Did you get to chase a Frisbee? Did you?"

Tyler picked up the shorts and dropped them again. "What's going on here? You're leaving?"

"Just going over to Lexie's," Jason said, folding the shorts and putting them in the suitcase. She had a state-of-the-art laundry room. If he needed to wash some clothes, he could.

"Oh? Did you get back together?"

"Nope." Jason popped the P, trying not to think about holding her hand and sleeping with her curled into his side on the couch. "She hired me to be her bodyguard."

"Ah." Tyler didn't press the issue, and Jason didn't look at him. He'd mentioned in passing once that he'd dated Lexie a long time ago. Nothing specific, and Tyler wasn't the type to press or gossip. Thankfully.

"Thanks for coming to get Steve last night."

"Anytime, man." Tyler sat in the recliner, obviously in no hurry to leave.

Lexie came through the back door just as Jason finished packing and zipped his suitcase closed.

"It's so beautiful here," she said, turning back to look out the window. "The beach, the trees. I don't have a view like this."

Jason did love his beach hideaway. It wasn't anything fancy—Tyler at least had a separate bedroom at his place—

but it was all Jason needed. Or so he thought. One look at Lexie, and he knew he needed more.

"It is nice." He took two steps into the kitchen and started collecting food for Steve.

Lexie turned to face him. "Maybe we should stay here."

He abandoned the food bowls and leashes in favor of staring at her. "What?"

Tyler stood, and Lexie's eyes darted to him. "Oh, hey, Tyler. I didn't see you there."

"Just brought Steve back. Let's go, Bones." He caught Jason's eye as he moved toward the front door. "Good luck, man," he muttered, pulling the door closed behind him with a very final snap.

When Jason met Lexie's eyes again, he found a flush in her face. It only endeared her to him further, and he twisted his fingers through the leash as he said, "Tell me why you think we should stay here."

NINE

LEXIE'S PULSE filled her whole chest, making her throat narrow and speaking impossible. She shrugged instead, knowing that wouldn't fly with Jason. It never had. He'd always wanted her to talk to him, tell him what she wanted. And then he thought about it before reacting. It had been one of the most attractive things about him when she'd been with him before.

Still was, and she wondered how long she could fight her growing feelings for the gorgeous man in front of her.

"It's just," she started, her voice scratchy and weak. She cleared her throat, reminding herself that she was Lexie Keller, a billionaire heiress who ran one of the largest investment firms in the world.

"Victor already knows where I live," she said. "But he doesn't know where you do. Maybe this is the smarter option." Maybe if she played this about being smart and safe, she could hide how she felt about Jason a little longer.

They hadn't kissed after their lunch date, but it was all Lexie could think about. Gazing over the bay a few minutes ago, she let herself fantasize about what it would be like to open that door again, walk through it with Jason's hand in hers, and embrace how she felt.

"This is six-hundred square-feet," Jason said, his tone unreadable. "Look around, Lex. This is what this is. There's no bedroom. There are two doors here, and one leads to a bathroom and one to a closet." He swept his arm around the shack, but Lexie didn't look away from him.

"Are you embarrassed that this is where you live?" she asked.

"No." Jason shook his head, frustration brewing in his eyes. "Not at all. I'm just wondering where you think you'll sleep."

"There's a hammock in those trees back there."

"And you think sleeping outside will be safer than in your fortress?"

Lexie cringed. "Is that really what you think of my house?"

Jason shook his head again, returning to his chore of packing up the supplies he needed for his dog. "This conversation is getting off-track." He looked at her. "Your house is beautiful. Wonderful. Big, with sturdy locks." He turned his back on her and bent to get something out of a lower cupboard. "This place is none of those things."

"But Victor doesn't know where it is."

"He wouldn't know if you stayed in a hotel either," Jason said, filling a gallon-sized zipper bag with dog food. "And there are dozens of them in Getaway Bay. You could move to a new one every night. I mean, if we're talking about how to disappear and stay safe."

Lexie cocked her head, hearing something in those last words. "What does that mean?"

Jason sealed the bag and set it aside, his preparations apparently done. "It means, Lex, that I've done that. Moved around. Hopped from hotel to hotel to avoid…certain things. If that's all you need, let's get you into a hotel right now."

When considering Victor, yes, all Lexie needed was to stay somewhere safe he didn't know about. But considering everything else….

"I don't want to go to a hotel," she said. "I want—" She couldn't say what she wanted. Could she?

Something dangerous entered Jason's eyes and he came around the counter which he'd kept between them. "What do you want, Lexie?" He practically purred her name, and Lexie had very few defenses left.

Throwing all caution to the wind, and her hands up into the air, she blurted, "I want you, Jason. Okay? I want to be with you again, and have you tell me everything that happened, and see if we can make a life together on this island." Her chest heaved and yet she couldn't get a decent breath.

He stood there, his tiny dining table between them, his expression storming like a hurricane.

"Say something," she said.

"I don't know what to say."

"You're off the clock," she said. "And maybe that doesn't matter. Maybe we'll just spend time together, and talk, and Victor won't be able to get near me." Win, win, win.

Jason took another step toward her. "You want to talk?" He continued to advance, taking both of her hands in his. "Just talk?"

Lexie couldn't look away from his mouth. "Yes," she whispered. "Don't you think we need to talk?"

Jason swept his mouth across her temple, moving his hands from hers to her waist. "We can talk," he said, his lips skating down to her earlobe. Everything inside her went weak, and she grasped onto his shoulders, almost desperate to kiss him now.

Lexie's brain felt slow, sluggish, with Jason's scent so prominent and his hands on her body. All at once, she realized what she was doing, and she stiffened.

Jason noticed, because he stepped back, taking his touch with him. "So, talking." He cleared his throat and returned to the kitchen. "I have to work at Sweet Breeze tonight, so I'd love a nap between now and then. But we could order in for dinner and relax in that fancy loft of yours."

Lexie didn't think her loft was anything special, but Jason had had one in his place in New York, and she supposed it probably reminded him of that. "That sounds good," she said. "What can I help you get?"

"How do you feel about taking Steve?" He held out the dog's leash, and while Lexie had never been that big of a fan of canines, Steve panted on the couch without a care in the world. She had serious doubts about how her cats would get along with him, but they didn't live in the house and well, Steve obviously did.

"I can get Steve." She took the leash from Jason without touching his fingers and clipped it to the dog's collar. "Come on, Steven. Let's go."

Jason chuckled as he tucked the food and a couple of other things into a small box and then picked up his suitcase. "Steven? Is he in trouble?"

"He seems more like a Steven." Lexie glanced over her shoulder to find Jason right behind her. He walked out without locking the door behind him, and Lexie really wished she could spend more time in his little house. It felt comfortable, peaceful, and a distant memory surged forward of how much she'd enjoyed spending time at his apartment in New York City.

Once everyone and everything was loaded into her car, Jason got behind the wheel and eased out of his sandy driveway. She took another look at his tiny house, a pang of longing still pulling through her.

"Should we grab something to eat right now?" He turned onto the paved road and headed toward town. "We could get some of those take-home pizzas for later. Salad." He cut a glance at her, but she couldn't see his eyes behind the shiny shades. "You like salad."

"I do like salad. And the grocery store over on Vine has a take-home salad bar."

"Oh, that sounds dangerous." He grinned and reached over to take her hand in his. "Let's go there. Load up for tonight and tomorrow."

"Sounds like you're not planning on leaving the house."

"I'm not. Well, I have to work tonight." The light turned red and Jason slowed to a stop. "I think I'll call in though. I don't feel comfortable leaving you the first night after Victor followed you home."

Anxiety crawled through Lexie too, but it wasn't because of Victor. "Owen made it sound like he really needed you to valet."

Jason's jaw tightened, but he didn't argue. Which meant Lexie was right, and he couldn't call in and skip work. "Maybe I'll come hang out with you," she said.

"Victor is a guest at Sweet Breeze. You think it's smart to go right where he is?"

"Luke should've delivered the restraining order today," she said. She pulled out her phone and texted him. "I'll find out." Lexie couldn't help thinking she didn't really need a bodyguard, but she couldn't bring herself to say so. She wanted Jason upstairs, in her kitchen, at her side.

Drake never got back to me. Luke's text didn't settle Lexie's worries. *I'll call him right now.*

But it was almost eight o'clock in New York, which meant the reminder that Victor couldn't come within fifty feet of Lexie wouldn't go out until tomorrow at the earliest.

"The lawyer never called Luke back." Lexie frowned at the shops and buildings buzzing by. "I'll call Owen. Maybe he can get someone else."

Jason practically knocked her phone out of her hand. "Lexie, I can take care of my own job. I can call Owen myself."

A sting pinched her lungs. She got a firm grip on her phone and glared at Jason. "Okay. You don't have to swat at me."

"I just don't need you taking care of my business."

He'd never liked that, and foolishness raced through Lexie. "All right. I know. Sorry." And she meant it.

"I didn't mean to swat you," he said quietly as he pulled into the grocer on Vine. The tension between them intensified for a moment, and then Lexie released her breath.

"I'm sorry, Lex."

"It's okay." She tried on a smile and it seemed to fit okay. "Let's go get what we need." She reached for the door handle, but he put his hand on her thigh. Fire reared and raced through her, though his skin wasn't even touching hers.

"Let me get out first, okay?" He didn't wait for her to answer before he got out and closed the door.

"Is he always like this?" she asked Steve, but she already knew the answer. She'd hired him to be her bodyguard, and he was going to do exactly that. He scanned the parking lot, but all Lexie could see were moms walking in or out with their kids. The later crowd on Friday night would be couples and teens, but for now, everything looked safe.

Jason finally opened her door, right when Lexie felt like panting as hard as Steve was. "All right," he said. "But we stay together in the store." He moved to the back door and let Steve out, his leash tight around his hand. "Right next to me, Steve."

The dog complied, and even Lexie wouldn't have dared disobey him when he spoke in that voice. He hadn't changed into one of the expensive suits she'd bought, but he looked formidable and imposing anyway.

They moved through the store like they were on a covert mission and continued on to her house. Jason didn't relax until the garage door closed behind them and he locked the entrance into the house after that.

He unclipped Steve, who started sniffing everything in sight, while she took their groceries into the kitchen.

"I'll be right back," he said, his phone already at his ear. She nodded and heard him say, "Owen, hey, it's Jason Burnes," before he disappeared upstairs with his suitcase.

Lexie usually liked the quiet atmosphere of her house, but today it felt oppressive. She went outside to feed and water the cats. Steve came with her and if Brownie or Slinky were around, they didn't come out with the spaniel's presence.

"You can stay out here," she told the dog, and he did, happily sniffing her trees, bark, rocks, and fountain grass. She left the door ajar for him and went about unpacking the groceries. When her phone chimed a message from Sasha about meeting at the beach, Lexie's first inclination was to say *Yes! Be there in twenty.*

Then she remembered who was upstairs and what they had planned. She couldn't make him go sit on the beach at a healthy distance while she chatted with her new beach friends.

I wish I could! she sent instead. *I've hired a bodyguard and we're working out some details.* That sounded really professional and not like she'd hired her previous boyfriend to stay in her upstairs bedroom, bake pizza for her, and skip out on his job that night because she was afraid to stay in her own house alone.

Who did you hire? Of course Sasha would ask, and Lexie didn't see how she could keep it a secret.

Jason.

She expected Sasha to call, as the woman wasn't a fan of texting long messages. So when five hearts in various colors came in, all Lexie could do was smile.

"Who are you texting?" Jason asked, sweeping into the kitchen smelling like fresh cotton and cologne.

Lexie flipped her phone face-down on the counter as Jason walked past. "You showered?"

"I slept in my clothes last night." He indicated the fridge. "Do you have water in here?"

"Yes, sir."

He opened the fridge and retrieved a bottle. He offered it to her first, but she declined. He was so strong, so sensitive, and yet so sexy too. Lexie sighed, only realizing when he looked at her and quirked one eyebrow that it had been a very, very loud sigh.

A happy sigh. A content sigh. A come-kiss-me sigh.

"Are we napping first?" she asked, hoping to cover up the sound she'd made. "Or do you want to put a movie on? Go for a walk?"

He took a long drink from his bottle and then set it on the counter. He stalked closer, and Lexie had seen that look on his face before.

"Jason," she warned.

"Hmm?" He wrapped his arms around her and dipped his head toward her ear. "I heard that sigh, Lex. I've heard it before."

Of course he had.

She giggled and felt daring and like someone she hadn't

been for a long time when she said, "So what comes next, smarty pants?"

Jason somehow brought her closer, his hands hot and tight along her waist. "This." He brought his mouth to hers, kissing her like he'd been thinking about doing it for seven years. Like he'd never gotten over her, as he'd claimed. Like she was his and would never be anyone else's.

Lexie kissed him back, trying to pour as much passion into her touch as she felt in his.

TEN

JASON COULD NOT BELIEVE he'd gone from standing behind a tree, watching Lexie hand drinks to customers to standing in her kitchen kissing her in only two days.

He couldn't believe he'd waited so long to contact her. Couldn't believe she was kissing him like she needed him to keep breathing, keep living. But the way she pressed herself into him and prolonged the kiss, Jason felt like the last seven years hadn't even happened.

He finally slowed the kiss and pulled back, his heart racing like he'd been running for a long time. "Okay, wow." He held her close to his chest, everything he'd ever hoped for. Well, almost. He still had to tell her what had really happened.

She giggled and buried her face in his shirt. "Wow?"

"Yeah." He stepped back and picked up his bottle of water. "I'm too old to beat around the bush." He finished the rest of the water. "I told you I'd never gotten over you. The only reason I haven't tried to get you back earlier is because I didn't know where you were."

Lexie reached up and pushed his hair off his forehead. "And you were bouncing around in hotels."

So she wanted to go there right now. "For a little while," he hedged. "Didn't last long. There's always another story for reporters, you know?"

"Is that why you went into journalism?"

Jason couldn't really name why he chose the jobs he did. "It was something I hadn't done before," he said. "I found I was good at writing. My PI experience allowed me to find the people no one else was interviewing." He shrugged. "And I wasn't afraid to ask questions until I got the answers I needed."

Plus, it had brought him to Hawaii when Tyler had gotten engaged. Jason had known from the first moment he'd laid eyes on Tawny and Tyler that the engagement was fake. All he'd had to do was wait for the right opportunity. Kind of like what he'd done with Lexie at Sweet Breeze the other night.

"So what do you do at Sweet Breeze?" he asked, moving around the huge island and settling at her bar.

"What do you mean?"

"I mean, you were there at nine o'clock the other night and didn't come down until almost midnight." He watched her, employing some of that patience he'd needed in his various careers.

"I had a meeting," she said, and Jason thought that was

only part of the truth. He wasn't sure he wanted to push it at the moment.

"Owen said he can call in a sub for me," Jason said, changing the topic.

"That's great." Lexie smiled at him. "Did you want to take a nap?"

"If we put on a movie, that'll put me out." He grinned back at her.

Instead of leading him up to the loft, Lexie went into the living room, which had a much larger TV, and she put something on she wanted to watch. Jason honestly didn't care, and he didn't think Lexie would really watch it anyway.

Sure enough, ten minutes into the movie, she said, "So you really didn't tell the papers about us?"

"I did not." He lifted his arm and drew her into his side. "I quit at the bar the moment they walked through the door." His mind flowed back to that day, and it had been a pretty awful day.

He should've expected it, what with the storm that Lexie and her firm were weathering. But he hadn't, and he'd had no choice and no chance to prepare himself.

"I texted Louis and said I wouldn't be coming back, and anyone else who came in asking about me he should just say I didn't work there anymore and he didn't know where I was."

Lexie laid her hand across his stomach, and all his muscles tightened then released. "I bounced around New York for about a week, and then I went to Miami. Got a job there working at a newspaper, and eventually I landed at Aces High."

"How do you think they found out about us?" she asked.

"Honestly?"

"Of course, honestly." She tipped her head back and looked at him.

Jason's jaw tightened and he wondered if he should say anything. In the end, he didn't want anything between them. "I think it was Luke."

"No." Lexie shook her head immediately. "He wouldn't do that. He didn't even know about us."

"Lex." Jason focused on the TV screen though he had no idea what was going on. "Luke is a lot of things, but stupid isn't one of them."

Lexie fell silent after that, and Jason wasn't sure what else he could say. His attention wandered, and he was tired, but he had one more thing to tell her.

"I didn't think you two needed to be at odds back then," he said. "So I was willing to take the fall. You should know that Luke has never come out and admitted to me that he told the press about us, but I got a text from him right after I got to Miami."

Lexie looked at him, waiting for more.

"It said 'Thanks for being a good friend. Sorry about how everything happened.'"

Tears gathered in Lexie's eyes, but she blinked them back and anger replaced the emotion. "I'm going to kill him."

"No." Jason eased her back into his arms. "It's over, Lex. What would the point be?"

"He said he hadn't spoken to you once."

"That's not entirely a lie. We didn't speak. I didn't even

respond to his text." Jason cleared his throat. "I did try to find you, once."

"You did?" She sat up again, and Jason wasn't sure he'd be able to fall asleep at this point. Talking usually took the energy right from his body, especially hard stuff like this.

"Yeah." He nodded, remembering how he'd tried to track her down using some of his detective, police, and private investigator skills. "I asked Bruce if he'd just give me a hint of where you'd gone. He wouldn't. Was pretty nasty about it too."

"So you just gave up, I'm sure," Lexie said, that sexy sarcasm in her voice.

"For a while," he said. "Then I started making phone calls here and there. You used to have secretaries and lunch dates and friends. But you'd seemed to cut everything and everyone off and just disappear. I thought I might not be able to find you."

"But you did."

"It was luck," he said. "Well, sort of. The day before Tyler's bogus engagement hit the newswires, I'd finally gotten your ex-fiancé's now ex-girlfriend to tell me that you'd gone somewhere tropical."

"That doesn't mean Hawaii."

"Sure didn't. But then I got Tyler's story, and I was on my way here already. The rest is just dumb luck. Or fate. Or divine intervention. Something."

Lexie had always been able to absorb a lot of information and process it quickly. She was as smart as she was sexy, and Jason felt like a weight had been lifted from him with all he'd said.

"Are you mad about me snooping into your life?" he asked.

"No. Well, maybe a little."

"It was a long time ago," he said.

"Besides you were hanging around at The Straw for months."

"Months? Come on." He chuckled. "I didn't even come to Hawaii permanently until mid-February." Two months. He felt better here among all the palms and sunshine than he ever had in New York City.

"Feels like longer."

"To me too."

A few minutes passed, and Jason felt himself coming down off the adrenaline high of revealing important things. He'd just closed his eyes when Lexie said, "I think it was fate that brought you here," she whispered, her lips touching his a moment after she finished talking.

Surprised, Jason's eyes flew open, but she kept kissing him, and he liked this kind of talking a lot more than any other type. He believed a lot could be said with a kiss, and Lexie was telling him she'd never gotten over him either.

After the best make-out session of his life, Jason did manage to fall asleep. He woke to a loud bang and Steve's booming bark and sat up, the living room dark—and Lexie gone.

He jumped to his feet, the light coming from the foyer making his eyes adjust to the darkness in a strange way. When a wash of headlights swept across the large window in the living room, Jason called, "Lex?" at the same time he ran to the front door. Steve stood a few feet away, snarling. He looked at Jason for a brief moment and barked again.

She didn't answer and Jason whipped open the front door. Steve launched himself out onto the porch, barking like a mad dog. Outside, Jason saw a car speeding off into the night. He cursed under his breath that he'd been asleep when he should've been bodyguarding—he wasn't even going to valet tonight. He shouldn't have been napping.

Lexie yelped from inside the house, and Jason turned that way at the same time something acrid met his nose. The light spilling from the house illuminated smoke rising from Lexie's front lawn. Panic built in Jason's chest, and he darted back into the house and headed straight for the kitchen.

"Fire extinguisher," he said, his breath sticking in his throat as Steve continued to bark outside. He yanked open the cupboard under the sink, sure Lexie would have the proper gear in her kitchen. She was nothing if not detailed.

"What's going on?" she asked.

He spied the red fire extinguisher and pulled it out, knocking over several bottles of cleaners and soaps in the process. "Someone was just here," he explained quickly. "There's something smoking on the front lawn." He started back toward the open front door, but paused and turned back. "Stay here."

Lexie wrung her hands together, but thankfully, she stayed put. Jason nodded and headed back to the lawn. Beside the door, there were several light switches. Jason flipped them all, thankfully flooding the front of the house with light. Steve stood on the edge of the wide porch, barking at everything in front of him.

There was no fire, just a steady stream of smoke that smelled like rotten eggs lifting into the sky. In the bright light from Lexie's house, it looked like blue smoke, and Jason found the smoke bomb on the lawn easily.

He kicked it out of the grass and into the rocks just as another car came down the quiet lane. He had no idea what time it was, but the car slowed enough to tell Jason that the two men driving by weren't here for a social visit.

They both had dark eyes and hair, and wore equally menacing looks. Steve dashed down the yard and stood in front of Jason, his bark so loud, Jason could barely hear himself think. His heart was in a contest to beat as loudly as Steve was barking.

Jason made his shoulders boxy and lifted the fire extinguisher like he could do some real damage with it. His message was clear: *Keep moving, boys. She's not alone.*

The car did continue on, turning the corner at the end of the block before the roar of an engine filled the air and the car rocketed away.

Steve quieted, Jason relaxed and looked at the smoke bomb that had marked Lexie's house. So Victor couldn't get within fifty feet of her, but that didn't prevent him from sending a couple of goons to take care of the job.

Jason wasn't sure what "the job" entailed, but he now knew Victor Bunce wouldn't be backing down, restraining order or not.

A smoke bomb wasn't dangerous, so he left it where it was and returned to the house, noting a blue mark against the door—probably where the bomb had hit and then bounced into the yard. Probably also the sound that had woken him.

"Come on, Steve," he said to the dog still standing on the lawn as if daring another car to come by.

He entered the house, waited for Steve to sniff around and come inside, then closed the door behind him, locking it, and returning to the kitchen. Lexie wasn't there, but the bottles he'd knocked over had been cleaned up. He set the fire extinguisher on the countertop, noted the cooked pizza on the stovetop, and went to find the woman he was supposed to protect.

"Lexie?" he called, noting the back door was locked. As was her bedroom door. He knocked there, and said, "It's Jason, and they're gone."

A few moments later, she opened the door, her face stern and determined and yet seconds away from crumbling.

"It's okay," he said, taking her into his arms. She practically collapsed against him, and the heat from her tears singed his chest. He just held her, right there in the doorway to her bedroom, wishing none of this was happening. Wishing he could truly protect her. Wishing he hadn't fallen asleep like a pathetic snoozer.

"I'm sorry, Lex," he whispered over and over. "I'm so sorry."

ELEVEN

LEXIE ONLY ALLOWED herself to cry for a minute. Maybe two. Then she somehow gathered herself back together and straightened. Jason didn't let go of her as she wiped her eyes. "I called the police," she said, her voice much too high.

"You did?"

"You ran out with a fire extinguisher," she said. "Steve was barking his fool head off." The dog now sat at Jason's feet, utterly nonplussed.

"I'll go change." He started to ease away from her, but she latched onto his elbows.

"Change?"

"Yeah, I'm the bodyguard. I can't be wearing sweats. That's what the boyfriend does." He hurried around the steps and took them two at a time up to his bedroom. Lexie felt lost and alone, and even when Keller Investments had indictments against them, she hadn't felt like this. She'd had her family in her corner, a whole legal team, and Jason.

Until she didn't have him.

She'd been stewing over what he'd said for hours. *Luke* had told the press about her secret relationship with the bartender? How had her brother even known?

Jason had sworn up one side of the Mississippi and down the other that he'd never told Luke about Lexie, despite them being best friends.

She didn't have any more room to spare in her mind, but when Jason came downstairs wearing that gray suit.... Lexie could only think about how handsome he was, and how he hadn't hesitated at all with that fire extinguisher.

"You didn't have to change." She smoothed her hand down his lapel. "But this is hot."

"A bodyguard doesn't wear sweats and a T-shirt." He adjusted his tie and turned toward the front door as Steve got to his feet and gave a low growl in the back of his throat. "They must be here." He strode away, clearly going to handle the situation, for which Lexie was grateful.

But he seriously could've worn the sweats and the T-shirt, because he looked like a mafia boss in either outfit. She went into the kitchen, her appetite completely gone. By the time she finished with the police, she'd have to reheat the pizza anyway, so she left it where it was and went into the foyer, where Jason was just welcoming the cops.

He gave his version of events, and Lexie had very little to offer. She hadn't heard the smoke bomb hit the front door. The first she'd known of it, Steve had started barking and then Jason was in the kitchen, pulling stuff out from underneath the sink.

The cops made notes, got Jason's number, left their card, and collected the smoke bomb before they left.

Jason leaned against the closed front door, weariness plain on his face despite his two-hour nap. "You better go pack a bag, sweetheart." He stood and walked toward her, his new shoes making slapping sounds against her floor.

"What? Why?"

"We can't stay here. I'll get us a hotel." He pulled out his phone, and her fantasies of having a Secret Service look-alike as her bodyguard all came true. "Yes, hi, my name is Brian DeLuth and I need two rooms for tonight. Do you have anything?"

Brian DeLuth? she mouthed, and Jason waved at her and turned away. She giggled, though nothing about having to pack a bag and go to a hotel was funny. She'd just returned to her bedroom to pack when Jason said, "I need a card, Lex."

"Oh, right." She hurried into the kitchen and pulled her purse off the built-in desk. She handed him her credit card and he hesitated.

"You know what? Can we pay in cash when we get there? Yes…yes, we're on our way. Adjoining rooms…thank you."

Lexie's heartbeat pumped a few extra times, and she dashed back into her bedroom to pack. Within ten minutes, Jason was turning back onto the highway that would lead them into town. And ten minutes after that, she'd gotten as much cash from her credit card as the ATM would allow and they stood at the check-in desk at Sunshine Sleep Inn, a rinky dink hotel across the street from the east bay.

Jason entered her room first and ushered her inside. He went next door and opened the doors connecting their room. "I don't think this will be necessary," he said. "But I wanted to have it just in case."

Lexie nodded, mourning the loss—the sanctuary—of her own home. She wandered over to the window, but the view was the building next door, and she promptly pulled the curtains closed again. The only place to sit was the bed, so she perched on the end of it, all the happenings of the day flowing through her like water over a cliff.

Exhaustion hit her at the same time her stomach growled. It must have been loud enough for Jason to hear, because he said, "I'll get you something to eat," and disappeared back into his room.

Lexie didn't want to be alone. A tremor of fear moved through her, and she got up to knock on Jason's door. But she couldn't do that either. In the end, she turned the TV on low and climbed onto the bed until Jason returned with a pre-made salad and a huge pizza from the gas station across from Sweet Breeze. It wasn't the romantic Italian meal she'd had planned, but it would have to do.

He didn't stay very long, but he did tuck her into bed and kiss her with a fierceness she hadn't experienced from him before. "Knock or text," he said his voice almost as growly as Steve's had been. "Any time. Okay?"

She nodded, and he left, and she lay in bed for a long time, just thinking. What had he done with Steve? They'd just left him at her house. Would he sleep tonight? Why couldn't she fall asleep?

She thought of him next door, alone, and she wished she were brave enough to go crawling into his arms and sleep beside him the way she had in the loft the night before.

The next day, she woke early and went immediately to the door and knocked. Jason took several long moments before he answered, his hair mussed and his eyes still sleepy. "Hey," he said, smiling and leaning into the doorway. Once again he made a T-shirt and gym shorts look like an Armani suit.

"I'd like to go to the gym," she said. "I'm assuming you won't let me go alone."

"Nope. Let me put on some shoes." He walked half a step in front of her, he opened the door to the hotel gym, and he waited for her to choose her machine before positioning himself directly next to her.

She liked being with him, found his presence comfortable, but she still put in her earbuds and got the treadmill moving. She might let Victor push her out of her house for a night, but she would not fall apart over him.

Only a mile into her workout, her phone rang. Luke. Her fingers twitched to get it, but at the same time, she wasn't sure she was ready to talk to him. In the end, she paused the treadmill and answered the call.

"Hey," she said, her breath sounding in her own ears as she puffed into the phone.

"Catch you at a bad time?" he asked.

"I'm on the treadmill," Lexie said. "It's fine. Did you hear from Drake?"

"He's pulling the restraining order right now. He'll send it in the next half-hour."

Some relief bled through Lexie. She wanted to tell Luke about last night, but she didn't at the same time. "Hey," she said. "Have you heard from Jason Burnes lately?" She glanced at the man in question, who ran on the treadmill beside her. No headphones. No movie on his phone. He was like a man of steel and willpower.

He looked at her too, and she turned away.

"No," Luke said. "Why? Is he causing a problem too?"

Jason had never been a problem. Never. "No," she said, unsure of why else she'd bring him up. "I've just been thinking about him, and I wondered, you know, since you guys were best friends...." She let her words hang there, sure Luke would fill in the blanks.

"I haven't spoken to him in years," Luke said, his voice even as always. "And Lex...I don't know how to say this."

Lexie was sure she wouldn't like it. "Maybe don't say it then," she said. "But I'm a big girl, Luke, and I can make my own decisions."

"Not when it comes to him, you can't," Luke said. "He's not right for you."

Funny, every time Lexie thought about the man that was perfectly right for her, he bore Jason Burnes's face. "Why do you say that?"

"He's just...he didn't even finish college."

"So what?"

"So I just think—"

"He was your best friend. From *college*."

"From my party years," Luke said. "Think about that, Lex. Last I heard he was in Miami. Probably down there partying it up. He's not husband material."

"Yeah, well, few men are," Lexie snapped. Neither of her brothers had managed to tie the knot, so she wasn't sure what Luke was talking about.

"I thought you'd get over him," Luke said, almost thoughtfully, but it was hard to tell through the phone line.

Lexie stepped off the treadmill, annoyed when Jason slowed his. "I was in love with him, Luke, and you had no right to tell the press about us."

Silence came through the line, and Lexie didn't like it. Didn't like that Luke didn't immediately deny what he'd just been accused of.

When he finally said, "I didn't," Lexie didn't believe him.

"I have to go," she said when Jason's treadmill stopped. The man could scent her distress from a mile away, and she'd liked that once. "Let me know when the restraining order has been sent."

"I will."

"Great." Lexie hung up, already regretting the little tiff with her brother. With her parents gone, and the way she and Luke had structured the company, she had to be on speaking terms with him.

"Everything okay?" Jason touched her shoulder and Lexie turned into him, painting a bright smile on her face.

"Everything's fine. I need to go shower and get ready for work." She strode ahead of him, well aware that she was treating him badly, pushing him away, but not sure what to do about it.

When he put his hand on her door, preventing her from going into her room, he said, "Lexie, don't shut me out."

She looked up at him, her brain so full and nothing making sense. She pressed her mouth to his, glad when he seemed as hungry for her touch as she was for his. "Ready in an hour?" she asked.

He nodded and let her go inside her room alone. Her door slammed shut, and she waited for his to do the same. But it didn't. Surely he wouldn't leave her alone, and she pulled her door open again to find him still standing in the hall.

"You can go shower," she said, her heart simultaneously wanting to pull him closer and push him away. She wouldn't be able to live with herself if he got hurt because of her. She'd caused quite enough upheaval in his life, what with her company scandal forcing him to quit his job and lose his loft in New York City.

He looked at her simply, everything laid out between them. "One hour." He nodded behind her, and she retreated and closed the door again. This time, his door closed too, and she got in the shower having only completed half of her workout—at least physically. Mentally, she was already ready for bed again.

"So he's just going to sit at the table all day?" Sasha eyed Jason, who indeed had planted himself at one of the four tables situated in front of The Straw.

Lexie hovered in the back of the stand, her eyes also locked onto Jason. "Yes. I've had some trouble, and he's here to make sure I don't have any more."

Sasha turned away from him to face Lexie. "What kind of trouble?"

"Some old business troubles," she said. "My lawyer has sent over the restraining order. But we ended up at a hotel last night." Lexie sighed and brushed her loose hairs off her forehead. She normally didn't even *have* loose hairs. But the last thirty-six hours had her all out of sorts and wondering which was to go next.

Her feelings for Jason certainly didn't help clear her mind, but thankfully a couple stepped up to the stand, and Sasha didn't have time to ask. When another lull hit, Sasha said, "When Maddy gets here, I'm heading to the beach. You want to come?"

"I don't have any of my stuff."

"Me either. I just sit there in my work clothes." Sasha smiled at her. "All the ladies want you to come again. We're dying to know how Jason went from a stalker to your bodyguard…." She wiggled her eyebrows. "And maybe more."

Lexie didn't want to lie to Sasha, so she said, "I'd love to come, but you know Jason will be there too."

"Can he sit down the beach or something?"

"He'll probably melt in that suit." Lexie giggled, the navy suit definitely making him stand out among the others on the beachwalk and down on the sand.

Sasha joined her, laughing so loudly Jason turned his attention to them. Lexie waved to him and enjoyed the confusion as it pulled across his face and he lifted his hand uncertainly.

"He is *gorgeous*," Sasha said. "And you know, you could stay with me and Jasper any time you needed to. He lives in a gated community."

"Now that is a good idea," she said, pulling out her phone when it buzzed in her back pocket.

What's so funny? Jason.

Going to the beach later. Hope you brought sunscreen. She added a smiley face to the message that hadn't answered his question and sent it flying the twenty feet between them.

He looked up at her, alarm evident on his face, which only made her laugh again.

TWELVE

JASON TRAILED HALF a dozen steps behind Sasha and Lexie, who walked down the beachwalk at the pace of snails. He seriously didn't think people could walk this slow. But apparently two women who were talking could.

It actually warmed his heart to see Lexie interacting with another woman in such a friendly way. No wonder she loved working at The Straw. It got her out of her house and gave her a reason to interact with other people.

They laughed, and Jason refocused his attention on everyone walking their way, searching for any unfriendly faces coming from the direction of Sweet Breeze. It was sweltering and hot, and sweat ran down his back. Sitting on the beach in late April sounded like torture, but he'd do it for Lexie.

He'd slept little the night before, and the sun certainly wasn't going to help his mood or his lethargic attention.

He detoured as soon as he saw the redhead already

sunbathing on the sand on the edge of the private beach that belonged to Sweet Breeze. A stand of trees bordered the grass surrounding Sweet Breeze, and Jason might survive if he could stand in a patch of shade.

Lexie turned when she and Sasha reached the other woman, and Jason nodded at her from his position under a palm tree. His mind had never been his best friend, and this bodyguard gig was almost as boring as standing at attention next to the check-in desk while he completed his security hours at the hotel.

One by one, three more women arrived, and they chatted and laughed for a few minutes. Lexie spoke quite a lot, and Jason felt his skin crawling, a sure sign that she was telling all those club women about him.

But not a single one of them turned and looked at him so maybe not. Jason wasn't sure he cared. He and Lexie were dating. It wasn't a secret this time, and Jason actually wanted to shout about it anywhere he could.

She'd already tried to put more distance between them, and Jason didn't like the idea of her walking away from him completely for reasons unknown. And Lexie knew how to disappear. A woman with an iron will and a lot of money was a dangerous thing, and Jason would not lose her again.

As he sat in the shade, he wondered if he was in love with her. He had been seven years ago, and though they'd only been spending time together for three days now, he felt the same now as he had then.

So definitely in love, he thought, not needing the extra warmth as it traveled through him. A smile touched his mouth at the same time a bolt of fear struck him in the gut.

"She's not going to leave," he told himself as he watched her tip her head back and laugh. A woman didn't go around putting down roots only to rip them up, though he supposed she'd done it once before. What was to stop her from doing it again?

He gave himself a little shake, wishing the troubling thoughts would go as easily. He tried to focus on the people coming and going, watching as a group of young adults showed up with a volleyball. They started a game on one of the public courts, and their yelling gave him something to focus on so he wouldn't fall asleep. Between that and watching everyone who walked by, he managed to make it through the hour that Sasha and Lexie spent on the sand with their friends.

They returned to the drink stand, and Jason went through the line, needing something ice cold to cool himself down. "Something sour," he told Lexie when she cocked her eyebrows at him. "Not the mango one. I've had that one."

"You have?"

"I'll do Orange Sunrise for him." Sasha exchanged a meaningful glance with Lexie, who turned back to Jason.

"What?" he asked, sensing something.

"Sasha said we can stay at her and Jasper's place tonight. I think it would be much more comfortable than a hotel. Did you get us somewhere already?"

"No." He found it best to book a room as late in the day as possible, usually as he was checking in. "Where do they live?"

"Up in the hills," Lexie said. "Behind a gate."

Sounded great to Jason, and while he'd spent most of the

night desperately trying to find a way to keep Lexie safe, having something worked out for him was a relief.

Sasha handed him the drink, and he asked, "Are you sure we can stay with you tonight?"

"Of course," she said. "And Jasper has a goldendoodle who would love to swim with Steve."

"You have a pool?"

"Yep." Sasha grinned at him. "So go text Tyler, and Lexie can go with you now, if she wants."

"You don't need me?" Lexie lifted her eyebrows at her friend. "It's Saturday night."

"Macey's coming in."

"But three of us—"

Sasha clearly kicked Lexie, which silenced her. Jason grinned at them and then took a long drink of his smoothie, getting a blast of orange, as well as some strawberry and banana too.

"This is great," he said to Sasha, and she beamed at him.

Lexie said, "Let me wash up, and I'll be out in a minute."

Sasha waited for Lexie to take the few steps to the back of the hut and turn on the sink. Then she leaned forward, almost all the way out of the shack. "You take care of her," she said, very seriously.

Jason sobered, sure there was more to what Sasha was saying. "I will. I—"

"I've already texted Jasper, and he's expecting you." Sasha straightened and stepped back as Lexie returned. "Bye, girl." She hugged Lexie and Jason fell back a few steps so he could be ready when Lexie came outside.

An hour later, Jason had changed out of his sweltering and sweat-stained suit into a pair of swimming trunks. He sat on the pool deck with his legs dangling into the water, watching a pair of dogs splash and swim and bark. He had never seen Steve so happy, and it made his heart happy.

As did the curvy, beautiful woman who came out of the house wearing a pair of cutoffs that showed the tan length of her legs and a bikini top the color of ripe apples. It had thick straps and a high neck, but still sparked plenty in Jason's imagination.

"Hey, sweetheart," he said as she sat next to him and handed him a section of the sub sandwich they'd bought on their way out of town. "Thanks."

"Jasper's on his way down. Said he normally doesn't work on the weekends, but he had an emergency in one of his mines in Australia."

Jason nodded, immediately recognizing Jasper as one of the men who came and went at Sweet Breeze the way Lexie usually did.

Jasper wore a full smile when he came onto the pool deck. "Jason." They shook hands and Jasper dragged a lounger closer to the edge of the pool and sat down. "I'm so glad you guys are here. Stay as long as you want."

"Oh, we probably won't stay long," Jason said, taking another bite of his sandwich.

"We won't?" Lexie met his eyes and searched them for unspoken answers.

He swallowed and said, "Well, I don't know." He didn't

want to admit he didn't have a plan, but he honestly didn't. She'd hired him to keep her safe, and he was trying. Having somewhere to stay behind a gate was a great thing, and perhaps he should simply keep her here until everything with Victor was settled.

"So, how do you two know each other?" Jason asked, returning his attention to his sandwich. But he still saw Lexie glance back to Jasper.

"We're in a lot of the same circles," Jasper said vaguely.

"You mean she's rich and so are you." Jason wasn't blind. And the man managed diamond mines in countries around the world.

Jasper laughed. "Oh, I like him, Lex."

Lex. The name seared through Jason's ears, and he couldn't just let it go. "Lex?" He raised his eyebrows at his girlfriend.

"We went out a couple of times." She rolled her eyes. "It was nothing."

"Very boring," Jasper said. "No spark."

"None whatsoever." Their eyes met again, and Lexie started laughing. "I've never told you that."

"It was a mutual feeling," Jasper said, chuckling too.

Jason didn't understand that. Everything about Lexie made him spark, including the simple way she tossed her hair over her shoulder and gently kicked her legs in the water.

He finished his sandwich and decided to really get answers. "So do you guys have some sort of secret club or something? You two, and Tyler Rigby, and Fisher, and that pineapple plantation guy? And there's a woman too. Well-dressed. Brunette. Left with a man wearing the most expensive suit on the island. A billionaire's club."

Jasper scoffed like such a thing was preposterous, but Jason got his confirmation from the absolute terror on Lexie's face. A moment later, she laughed too, but it sounded more like a choking machine gun.

"No," Jasper said.

"Jasper," Lexie said. "He was a private investigator once."

"And a police officer," he said. "And a detective. And a journalist." He peered over his shoulder at the other man. "So I pretty much know when someone is lying to me." He flashed a smile that said *gotcha*.

A few minutes passed where neither of them admitted to anything. Lexie pulled her legs out of the pool and said, "I have to go make a phone call," and not thirty seconds later, Jasper got up too.

"I need to check on something," he said, his excuse to escape from Jason much less sophisticated than Lexie's.

"All right," Jason called after him, watching as the man practically scampered back into his house. Discontent ran through Jason. Lexie hadn't told him everything about her life, and while he reasoned that she shouldn't have to share all her secrets, he still didn't like that she had part of her life she hadn't even told him about.

Especially since he'd tried so hard to be truthful with her, about everything. *Well, almost everything,* he thought. He still hadn't mentioned anything about the Browns, though Lyndsey had been asking him about his move to the island.

Suddenly, the dogs paddling around the pool weren't all

that fun to watch, and Jason got up and retreated to one of the loungers that lined the pool. He laid it all the way flat and lay down, taking in a deep breath and then releasing it. His mind felt soft, but he remembered one more thing he needed to do.

He made a phone call to the policeman who'd left his card with Jason last night, a man named Carson. "We left the house," he said. "As you suggested. But I just want to make sure nothing happens to it while we're not there. If Victor or one of his men come back tonight, they could set it on fire or something."

"I'll make sure we patrol," Carson said.

"Are you on duty tonight?"

"Yes, sir. I'll personally see to it that we check on the property throughout the night."

"Thank you." Jason ended the call and finally fully relaxed. With Jasper and the gated community, Jason thought he could afford to take a nap and Lexie would be okay.

He kept jerking awake, thinking he'd heard something hit the door, and it wasn't until Jasper finally came back outside and said, "She's upstairs asleep," that Jason allowed himself to drift off completely.

THIRTEEN

LEXIE WASN'T ASLEEP, but she was very good at faking something when she needed to. At least with most people. If Jason had come to check on her instead of Jasper, he would've known immediately that she wasn't really sleeping.

Instead, she stood at the window in the bedroom Jasper had given her on the second floor and looked down at Jason lying on the lounger beside the pool.

Luke had texted to say the restraining order had been delivered without incident, and she'd sent back a quick message that simply said *thank you*.

She couldn't help wondering if she should cut Jason loose. She didn't truly need him as a bodyguard, not anymore. Not with the restraining order back in place. Surely Victor Bunce would leave the island immediately instead of opting to be arrested. He might be mad, but he wasn't stupid.

And she certainly didn't need Jason getting hurt because of her.

And while she'd never had a problem with the secretive nature of the Nine-0 Club, she hadn't anticipated keeping secrets from him. Jasper had argued that they weren't engaged, and therefore she didn't need to tell him anything.

So while all the married men in the club had told their wives about the nature of their meetings, Lexie wasn't quite to the relationship stage where she felt comfortable.

"Doesn't matter," she muttered, her hot breath steaming up the window. Jason had already guessed it. The man was so observant and brilliantly keen about things. He might play a valet, but he didn't miss a single detail of the men and women who came in and out of Sweet Breeze.

When Lexie had told Jasper that, his solution was to simply move the meeting somewhere else.

"Where?" she'd asked. "Can't have it at my house, and your place is now obviously out. And there's no way I could get away from him to even go to a meeting at this point."

"I'll tell the others," he said. "They might even be able to help with Victor. Fisher would kick him out of the hotel, if you wanted him to."

Lexie didn't know what she wanted, thus why she'd escaped upstairs to try to figure things out. She sat in the recliner in the room and tried to relax.

A while later, her phone chimed, rousing her from a doze. It was Jasper, asking her if Sasha had mentioned being late that night.

A tremor ran down Lexie's arms. *No,* she typed. *Is she not back yet?* The light beyond her window had dimmed considerably, and Lexie wondered if Victor had gone by her house and not found her there. So he'd gone to The Straw, hoping to catch her. What if he'd caught Sasha instead?

She couldn't endanger her friends. She wouldn't.

She'd left New York to spare herself. Could she leave Hawaii to spare others?

Someone knocked on her door, and she got up to answer it. Jason stood in the hall, fully clothed and obviously showered. "Can I come in for a minute?" He gazed evenly at her, and she knew exactly what would happen once the door closed behind him.

"Sasha's not back," she said.

"She just came in," he said, hooking his thumb over his shoulder. "Jasper's with her in the kitchen."

Lexie wanted to see for herself, but she also wanted to kiss Jason, maybe one more time before she took the next steps to keep him and everyone else she loved safe.

Loved.

The word bounced around inside her head. Was she in love with Jason Burnes?

She backed up, keeping one hand on the door, and Jason pressed into her personal space and past her.

She brought the door closed and barely had time to lock it before Jason swept her into his arms and pressed his lips to hers. She matched his kiss stroke for stroke, the forbidden nature of it as exciting as it had been all those years ago.

"You don't have to tell me about your club," he murmured, moving his lips to her neck. She held onto his shoulders and tipped her head back.

"It's not a big deal," she whispered. "Stuffy, boring meetings for billionaires." She didn't care what Jasper said. It wasn't like she was going to invite Jason to the meetings. "Business stuff."

"I like your business." He kissed her again, his urgency dying off quickly and his kisses turning sweet and gentle before he pulled away completely. "I still feel like you're retreating from me." He stroked her hair off her face and looked at her. "Am I right?"

Lexie sighed and tucked herself against his chest so she wouldn't have to look right into his face and lie to him. "No," she said. "I'm fine."

His chest rumbled with a laugh. "Lex, you can't lie to me."

No, she supposed she couldn't. Why she thought she'd be able to was a mystery. "I don't want you to get hurt."

"Lexie—"

"I don't want Sasha to get hurt. I wouldn't be able to live with myself."

"We're going to get this Victor thing sorted out, and then your life will go right back to normal."

Ah, and he was the liar now. She wanted to call him on it, tell him that he'd changed the course of her life for a second time, and she'd never be the same now that they were back together. The thought of losing him for a second time was enough to make her thoughts derail, and she worked to push the panic back.

"And while we're sharing secrets," she said. "Those women on the beach? They have a little club too."

"Oh? And you're just joining it?"

"As a matter of fact, yes. I guess it's a safe space for them.

It started off as all single women who were done with men, but four of them are married now."

"Hmm." He swayed with her. "And do you see yourself getting married, Lex?"

"Depends," she said, though she'd always wanted to get married, and she and Jason had already had the marriage conversation, the kid conversation. A long time ago, sure, and maybe things had changed.

He stepped back and held her at arm's length. "Depends? That doesn't sound like the Lexie Keller I know."

"I told you, I'm not the Lexie Keller you knew."

He gave her that sweet yet sexy smile, and asked, "If I was the one down on one knee with the diamond, do you see yourself marrying me?"

Lexie felt like she'd been struck dumb, because she had no idea what to say.

After several long seconds, he said, "It's okay, Lex. I can see your answer on your face." Before she could ask him how she'd answered, he kissed her again, and she imagined it to be the slow, sensual, passionate kiss they'd share as man and wife.

She and Jason hung around Jasper's house the following day. He and Sasha left to go hiking, one of their favorite activities, but Lexie wasn't what she would categorize as outdoorsy, and Jason didn't want to have to deal with the security in an unknown place. So they sat by the pool, and lay in the loungers and kissed, and by the time he suited up to go to his job at Sweet Breeze, Lexie had thoroughly confused her bodyguard with her boyfriend.

Jason had told her that he'd discovered that Victor had come to Getaway Bay with his family for a routine vacation. But he'd seen Lexie, and sent his family back to New Jersey. He'd stayed, and he had no plans to leave that Jason had been able to find.

"Owen said he's on a day-to-day at the hotel, and he has to let them know the night before if he'll be checking out the following day. I've asked him to alert me as soon as that call comes in."

Jason seemed to think Victor would simply give up, but Lexie wasn't so sure. They had cops driving by her house day and night to make sure it didn't get vandalized. She'd been forced to relocate. It didn't sound like Victor was simply going to give up and go away.

As she waved to Jason from the front porch, she considered simply calling Victor and asking him how much it would cost to get rid of him. But Luke had been adamant years ago that Keller Investments didn't pay unless the courts said they had a legal obligation to do so. And the ruling had been in their favor in this particular case that Victor had already tried to win.

But is it worth it? Lexie wondered, securing the huge wooden door behind her. Jasper and Sasha had not returned from their Sunday-funday activities, and his house suddenly loomed around her, a menacing presence she didn't like.

And she couldn't leave.

She wanted to talk to Luke again. Find out what had

really happened all those years ago. She believed Jason, she did.

He's not right for you.

He's not husband material.

Lexie wanted to shake Luke's words out of her head, but they'd been plaguing her since yesterday morning, when she'd last spoken with him.

She'd just wandered into the kitchen when the doorbell rang. Her feet froze to the floor, and she had no idea what to do. This wasn't her house. There'd be no way for the visitor to even know someone was home. Still, she held very still as if the slightest movement from her would trigger an alarm and alert the person outside to her presence inside.

Her phone sounded then, and she cringed as she slipped it out of her pocket. Luke had messaged: *I'm on the front porch. Come let me in.*

She squinted at the words, trying to get them to make sense. The doorbell rang again, and loud banging accompanied it. She scampered to the threshold of the kitchen and looked toward the front door across the vast lobby.

Jasper said you'd be at his house, Luke's next message read. *Are you there or not?*

Without answering, Lexie started toward the front door. She guessed she was about to have a talk with her brother, whether she wanted to or not. She opened the door, almost expecting to see Victor and his goons and not her brother. Then again, if they used smoke bombs, maybe they weren't sophisticated enough to hack into a phone account and impersonate her brother.

"Luke," she said, the taller version of her father swimming before her eyes. She blinked and his dark features came into focus. "You need a haircut."

He grinned at her and gathered her into a hug. "And you sound like Mom."

Lexie laughed as she embraced her brother. "What in the world are you doing here?"

"I—You sounded distressed when I called yesterday. I wanted to come check on things with Victor. It's my understanding that he's still in town."

"He is." Lexie stepped back into the house. "How did you know where I was?" True, Luke might have more resources than Victor, but she didn't want to be traceable at the moment.

"You've mentioned Jasper a time or two," he said. "I think you went out with him a while ago? Anyway, he's got a unique name, and it didn't take our cyber team long to get a number for him. I talked to him this morning before I boarded my plane."

Lexie nodded, so many words piling up behind her tongue. "You always did have a good memory."

Luke flashed her a smile. "So this is where you're hiding out." He cast his eyes around the place, with all the high-end wood finishes and twenty-foot ceilings. "I gotta say, Lex, it could be a lot worse."

Like your brother lying to you for seven years. She cleared her throat. "It could." She indicated the living room, and Luke went that direction, only a briefcase in his hand. He wore a dark suit, and he probably slept in one too.

"Luke, I need you to tell me what happened seven years

ago." She sat down and folded her arms, ready to listen, her mind and ears wide open.

He exhaled and glanced around. "Do you think Jasper has anything to drink? This time difference is no joke."

"I don't know," Lexie said, her voice hollow. "You drink?"

Their eyes met, childhood memories flowing between them freely. "Only a little," he said. "When I'm stressed. It relaxes me."

"You're stressed? People come to Getaway Bay to you know, get away from it all."

"Yes, well, I came to tie up some business." He cocked one eyebrow and smiled at her. It had been so long since she'd seen him, actually been face-to-face with him, and her heart swelled.

"So seven years ago," he said. "The housing market crashed, because there were financial institutions that loaned money to people who couldn't pay it back."

Lexie waved him into silence. "Not that." She looked right into his dark eyes so like her own, only a hint lighter. "I need you to tell me why you told the press about me and Jason."

Luke's eyes widened and his mouth worked but no words came out. She simply watched him, waiting, while he composed himself.

"I already told you I didn't," he finally said.

"But I have it from an excellent source that you did."

"Who?" Luke challenged.

"Jason Burnes. Said you texted him later about how you were sorry about how it had to go down."

Fear, true fear, entered her brother's eyes. "Lex, you have to understand what things were like at the time."

"I know what things were like at the time, Luke. My name was on all the indictments. *Mine,* not yours."

"Exactly," he practically spat, his patience clearly gone already. "*Your* name. *Your* reputation. It couldn't be attached to his."

"Why not?"

"He's not who you think he is."

"He's exactly who I think he is."

Luke shook his head. "Jason's really good at playing a part, Lex. The bartender. The party animal. The artsy, loft-living guy who just wishes he had enough money to fill his place with paintings about people and their feelings."

"He was your best friend."

"I felt sorry for him. That's the only reason I brought him around for holidays. He had nowhere else to go, and no one should be alone at Christmas, you know?"

Confusion raced through Lexie. She'd felt like this before about Jason—like she'd spent all this time with him, had fallen in love with him—only to discover that she hardly knew him.

But that was when she'd believed *he'd* told the newspapers about them. Now that she knew—she suspected—that he hadn't, she didn't know what to believe.

"Lex, why are you so hung up on him?"

"He's here on the island," Lexie said, her voice coming out as a whisper. She wasn't sure why, only that she didn't seem to have the energy to make it louder. She wanted to tell Luke she was in love with Jason, and he wasn't her father and couldn't keep them apart. She pressed her lips together and looked at Luke. "Who is he?"

"You'll have to ask him, Lex." Luke shook his head. "I'm here to make sure Victor Bunce disappears from our lives for good."

"How are you going to do that?"

Luke unlatched his briefcase and pulled out a folder. "Write him a check."

Lexie listened to him detail how they'd be meeting with Victor in the morning and that by lunchtime, everything would be over. But Lexie couldn't help wondering if she'd lose everything this time the way she had last time—all by noon tomorrow.

FOURTEEN

"WHAT DO YOU MEAN, I'm not invited?" Jason didn't care that his cereal was getting soggier by the second.

"Just that." Lexie wouldn't look at him. She'd barely let him touch her when he got home from work an hour ago, and his brain felt sloppy and sluggish after a night of standing at the valet podium.

"Luke's in town, and we're going to handle it."

"What are you going to do?" Jason asked. "Pay him off?"

Lexie's gaze flitted around the room like a butterfly trying to find the perfect flower to land on. Jason groaned and wanted to shove his cereal away. "Lex, that's not a good idea."

"Why not?"

"How many more people will come looking for a payoff? What if he asks for more next year? Or the year after that?" Jason shook his head. No, in his experience, dealing with angry customers was never easy, but paying them off was also never the answer.

"Luke has legal paperwork," Lexie said, and he hated that everything about her was exactly where it should be. Not a hair sat out of place though it was only seven-thirty in the morning. Her makeup was flawless and added accents to her face he hadn't seen before. She wore a deep blue skirt set that flared at the knee. A pure professional, and he liked her in these clothes as much as the short shorts and halter top from the pool.

But he really didn't like that she'd paid so much attention to such details. And he wanted to rage that she was not going to meet with Victor by herself. "I'm coming," Jason said, a note of finality in his voice. "You owe me that much."

Lexie finally looked at him, doubt and desire and determination in her gaze at the same time. "Why would I owe you that?"

"I should get to face Luke, at the very least."

"You can do that after the meeting."

"When's he flying out?"

Lexie scraped butter onto her toast though the bread had cooled long ago. "I'm not sure."

"Liar."

Lexie lifted her eyes to his again. "Fine, he's got a flight out at three-ten."

"Wow, nice of him to stay for twenty-four hours." Jason didn't mean to bite the words out, and by the sour look on Lexie's face, she didn't appreciate it. But Jason tasted desperation in the back of his throat. He felt so out of control, like if he didn't go with Lexie to the meeting, he'd lose her all over again. That she'd be on the three-ten flight, buzzing out of his life to destinations unknown, and he couldn't stomach the thought of being without her for another seven years.

"Jason—"

"Please. Just let me drive you. I'll stay in the car."

"We're meeting at Sweet Breeze."

Of course they were. Everything seemed to happen at Sweet Breeze, and Jason was actually glad he was stationed there. "Great. I'll hang out with Sterling."

Lexie didn't argue after that, but he could tell she wasn't happy with the arrangement. Jason wasn't either, so at least they agreed on something.

The ride over to the hotel was silent and tense, and Jason wished he could do something about it. He pulled into the bay and waved at Sterling, and then proceeded to take the car to valet parking himself. He knew the system.

"What else did Luke say?" Jason asked once they'd parked and neither of them had made a move to get out.

Lexie turned her eyes on Jason and blinked those long, black lashes at him. "He said you're not who I think you are." Challenge lifted her eyebrows. "What does that mean?"

Jason swallowed, knowing exactly what that meant. He owed her the truth and had wanted to give it to her for seven years. From the moment they met, actually.

But some things were still too painful to talk about, even two decades later. "I have an idea," he said, hoping vague would work for now. "Your meeting is going to start in ten minutes."

Lexie still didn't budge. "They can wait."

"Are you sure?" Pure fear gripped Jason's insides.

"Jason." She sighed. "I think what we have is great. Once this is all over, I want to talk diamonds and children and how I'm going to be able to put up with Steve in my house. So I think I better know who you are before that happens."

Jason's hopes soared as high as the clouds, spiraling around like a happy little bird. She'd just said everything he'd been hoping for, praying for, and yet he knew that what he said next could ruin it all.

"People change, you know?" He looked out the window.

"I know."

But did she? She'd been raised with a silver spoon in her mouth, and while she worked hard for her success and money, it wasn't the same thing as how he'd clawed his way back from the gutter.

Literally.

Just say it, he told himself. *Tell her.*

"When I turned twenty-one, my friends at college threw me a big party." He felt himself turning off the emotions, smothering the guilt, escaping from himself. "I drank too much." He didn't let himself look at her as she inhaled sharply.

"You told me you didn't drink."

"When I met you, I didn't." He blinked, finally letting all the memories off the shelves where he'd kept them for so, so long. "And the reason I didn't—and still don't, and have been sober for seventeen years—is because I got behind the wheel of a car while I was intoxicated and I hit someone."

"No." Lexie sounded like he'd just told her he was the Grim Reaper and he'd come for her soul. Her fingernails made horrible noises on the door handle as she tried to grip it. "No, Jason."

"A family," he continued. "Two kids. Everyone survived, but there were some injuries. I got arrested. I spent some time in rehab and counseling. I got sober, and I left Boston and haven't been back."

Lexie didn't say anything but she also stopped trying to flee from him. He'd have to take that as a good sign, because there weren't many others.

"I send them cards still, at Christmas and dumb stuff like Easter. They—" His voice betrayed him and his throat closed off.

Lexie opened the car door, said, "I have to go," and got out. He couldn't tell if she slammed the door so hard his teeth rattled on purpose or not. Didn't matter. He didn't turn his head and watch her walk away, because he didn't want that visual in his mind. Not again.

"They advocated for rehab and an alcoholism treatment program instead of prison, and they send me stuff too," he finished. "On my birthday and every year on the anniversary of the accident. They're the kind of family I wish I'd come from. The kind of family I hope to build—with you."

He'd never told her this ugly truth about himself before, because she'd made such a big deal about him being a dry bartender. Said how much she admired him for that. As he'd grown to learn her past, he'd shoved his further and further away. He wanted to be the perfect man for her, but he'd always known way down deep that he could never be that person.

Luke had known. So when Jason had learned that he and

Lexie's relationship had been splashed all over the Internet and front pages of the tabloids after the housing crash, he'd known it was Luke. Known why he'd done it—so people would go after Jason and not Lexie. So her name would be cleared. So she could focus on rebuilding the company without a once-drunk at her side.

And Jason had been just enough of a coward to allow it.

Time didn't seem to have meaning, and he wasn't sure how long he sat in the car. Eventually, his body told him that it was much too hot to continue brooding without air conditioning, and he got out and walked through the underground parking structure toward the valet podium.

Sterling wasn't there, but another man stood there with his valet ticket. "How can I help you, sir?"

The man turned, and recognition flashed in Jason's mind. He might forget a name, but he never forgot a face, and he'd seen this man's before. Recently.

"Do you work here?" the man asked, looking dubious. He had wide shoulders and at least sixty pounds on Jason, with his Polynesian heritage tattooed all over his forearms.

"I sure do." He extended his hand to take the ticket. "I can grab your car and be back in a jif." He wasn't sure where Sterling was, or why he felt like he needed to get this car for this man, but he did.

Relief cascaded through him when the man handed over the yellow ticket. Jason looked at it and plucked the correct set of keys from the peg behind the podium. "Be right back." He'd only taken three steps when sudden understanding slammed into him.

He'd seen that man before. Riding as a passenger in the

car the drove slowly, slowly, slowly by Lexie's, with blue smoke lifting into the air.

It took every ounce of control in him to keep walking. His step stuttered slightly, but no one but him would've noticed. As soon as he was out of sight, he broke into a run toward the car in the valet spot. He unlocked it and slid into the passenger seat, yanking open the glove compartment to get any information he could.

His chest tightened, and the air was so hot, so hot. He swiped open the camera on his phone and went snap, snap, snap on the registration documents, anything he could that could identify this man and tie him to Victor.

As if lightning had struck, Jason thought, *What if this is Victor's getaway car?*

And everything slowed once again. He carefully put everything back in the glove compartment and went around to the driver's side. He fired up the engine and fiddled with the air conditioning, the radio, the seat placement.

Finally, he drove back over to the bay, but Victor hadn't come out yet. Maybe this man—Tane Palu—really was here by himself, but somehow, Jason didn't think so. Still, he had no choice but to get out and give the man his car.

He did, falling back to the podium just as a group of men came out of the sliding doors. A blast of the air conditioned air inside Sweet Breeze hit Jason, and he said, "I'll get someone to help you. Just a moment," and ducked inside as quickly as possible. He didn't want to get caught retrieving cars for people when he needed to figure out where Lexie was having her meeting—and find Sterling. It was completely unlike the man to leave his post without a note.

He approached the check-in desk like a hurricane, drawing Owen's attention. The man, always so polished and poised, turned from the dark-haired woman he was talking to. She had a flush in her face, and if Jason didn't know better, he'd say Owen did too.

But he clasped his hands and said, "Jason, what can I help you with?" in that smooth, rolling voice he had.

"Do you happen to know where Lexie and Luke Keller are having their meeting?" He gazed straight into Owen's eyes, trying to communicate the urgency with which he needed to find them.

"Fisher gave them the conference room on the third floor," Owen said, flicking his eyes around the lobby. "Is everything okay?"

"I don't think so," Jason said darkly. "Remember what we talked about last week?"

"I do." Owen glanced at the woman still standing there. "I'm afraid I'll have to reschedule, Gina." He cleared his throat, and Jason wondered what was going on with the two of them. He'd seen that woman in Lexie's Beach Club, and she'd clearly cast her spell over Owen. Jason actually had two seconds to think *Good for him* before Gina left, her fingers trailing down Owen's arm and finally leaving his suit jacket.

Owen pulled on his sleeves and said, "I'll call the police."

"Probably a good idea." Jason turned away from the general manager, wanting to sprint up to the third floor but not wanting to miss Victor, Lexie, or Luke in the transfer. There was only one way in and out of this hotel, and staying by the door was probably his best bet.

"I'm going to be security at the door," Jason said.

"What shall I tell the police?"

"That we have a robbery in progress." Jason strode toward the huge, gaping doors and positioned himself on the near side, where most of the activity in the lobby took place. Lexie had certainly stolen his heart, but he didn't think the cops would care about that.

A few minutes later, Owen hung up and nodded at Jason, who was starting to doubt his instincts. He kept his eyes moving left and right, trying to find that one thing that was out of place.

It was very busy on Sunday morning, with guests checking out after their long weekends at the resort, and Jason wished the crowd wasn't quite so thick. A limping man caught his eye, and it only took Jason two seconds to identify Sterling.

"Owen," he called, abandoning his post. He pointed to Sterling, who was clearly confused and turning in a half-circle. "Call an ambulance. Move aside, please," he said in a commanding voice, somewhat surprised when people actually did.

He got to Sterling in five strides and touched his arm. "Sterling." His heart tore a little for the friend who'd trained him to be a night valet. "What happened?"

"I think someone hit me. I woke up in the bathroom." He lifted his hand to his head, and his fingers came away smeared with blood.

Jason passed the man to a couple of registration clerks, who whisked him away down the hall. Owen appeared, obviously concerned—and angry. "We need to clear the lobby," Jason said.

Owen didn't question him. Just lifted the radio to his lips and said, "Code pink. Lobby cleared. Non-panic. Fisher, I need you on the floor."

"Coming," Fisher said almost immediately, and the radio had barely silenced before someone said, "Confirming code pink. Additional personnel will arrive in thirty seconds."

Jason couldn't help being impressed with the efficiency of this hotel, and sure enough, men wearing suits and hotel uniforms spilled out of the stairwell doorway only seconds later.

Owen started directing them to set up ropes for in and out, and he himself moved over to the check-out counter. "Folks, we've got a situation in progress. I'm going to need you to move your line to the right. To the right, please." As they moved—it was like herding cats, if Jason were being honest—employees set up ropes to keep the line where they wanted it.

His phone chimed at the same time the elevator opened and four men darted out of it.

One of them was Victor Bunce, and he led the charge for the doors. Jason braced himself, knowing he was about to get hurt. Hopefully, though, Victor would as well.

He had just enough time to see the door to the stairs open again and Luke, Lexie, and an unknown suit sporting a bleeding lip burst into the lobby.

Then he threw a punch, hoping it was on target.

FIFTEEN

LEXIE FELT like she was watching a very bad movie. The director had slowed down the fight scene so that she could see every eyelash, every drop of sweat, every curled lip. She heard Jason's fist connect with Victor's jaw, saw the man's head snap back, saw Jason pounce on top of him and growl, "Stay down."

Somehow, she saw and heard all of that.

When life rushed forward again, the air was really full of screams and yelling. Luke ran off, followed by Drake. They wrested the satchel from the hands of one of Victor's goons, and Luke wiped his too-long hair off his forehead.

Lexie stood still, completely unable to move. So much had happened in the last twelve hours that she couldn't wrap her head around anything. She wanted to disappear on a nice, big boat and sail away from the island until everything made crystal clear sense.

Jason had Victor pinned, and he wasn't moving. All of

the men that had been with him had been apprehended, but Jason continued to bark orders and several men left through the glass doors to check something in the bay where guests arrived.

Policemen arrived, and Lexie sagged against the wall, beyond relieved that Jason had "waited in the car."

At the same time, her promise to herself never to be with an alcoholic reared, reminding her of what kind of man he really was.

Anyone who got behind the wheel of a car while drunk.... She shook her head, her tears filling her eyes so completely she wouldn't be able to wipe them before they spilled down her face. And then her perfectly crafted makeup would be ruined.

"Come on," Owen Church said, latching onto her elbow and leading her down the hall toward his office. "Wait here, Lex. I'm sure the cops will want to talk to you."

Luke will handle it. Lexie couldn't say the words, but Owen nodded at her and disappeared, closing the door and sealing her inside. Numbness spread through her, and though it wasn't particularly cold in Owen's office, she shivered as if she'd been encased in ice.

She should've had Jason in the room with her. Things had gone bad from the moment Victor walked in with four men to face her, her brother, and their lawyer. He hadn't cared about the legal documents, and he'd refused to sign.

He wanted a lot of money right now—over a million dollars—and more next summer. And every summer after that. So Jason had been right. Victor Bunce wanted to extort them, and he said he could continue to make life very difficult for Lexie on the island if she didn't pay.

Thankfully, she'd had a spine in the meeting, and she'd flat-out denied his requests. That was when one of the men left, and Luke had laid out what Keller Investments was prepared to offer. And he had half the money in cash, in the satchel that one of Victor's men had stolen. Victor had punched Drake, and they'd all fled.

It felt like everything had happened so fast, and yet had taken forever. Lexie trembled for a final time and then got up. She was the CEO of Keller Investments, and she needed to make sure the company was safe and sound. That they had their money and assets in order, and that there would be no more threats from Victor Bunce.

So she stood and straightened her skirt, her blouse, and her jacket, patted her hair, and opened the door to face the situation head-on. She'd taken four steps in her pristine heels when Jason rounded the corner, his face a perfect storm of emotions.

"There you are." He swept toward her, reaching for her, and she ached to find comfort in his arms. He paused and dropped his hands, his face falling and then bricking over as if a mask of stone had been poured over his emotions.

"The police need a statement." He hooked his thumb toward the lobby. "They've arrested Victor and his men. Apparently your lawyer taped the whole conversation."

Lexie nodded once as if of course she knew that Drake had recorded the meeting. "Thank you, Jason." She made to move past him, but he put his hand on her forearm.

"Is this where we are?" The pain in his voice sounded like a shriek, but she couldn't reassure him.

Employing her bravery, she looked up into his dark, dreamy eyes. "I need some time." When she walked away this time, she hoped it wasn't for the last time. She didn't look back at the corner though she could feel Jason watching her.

She faced the fray in the lobby, glad when a police officer guided her to a private room to make a statement.

When she returned to Sasha's house, her friend wasn't there but over at The Straw. Jasper was asleep, and the mansion felt like it might be the refuge she needed. But she couldn't stay there. She packed quickly and let her brother take her back to her own house. Now that Victor had been apprehended, as well as those he'd hired, she had no reason to stay somewhere else.

Guilt pricked her at leaving Jason to return to *her* friends' house and retrieve his things, and she'd have to get her car back from him at some point. But that was easy. Drop off and go. Or park it along the beachwalk near The Straw and she'd drive it home the next time she worked. She could catch a ride wherever she needed to go simply by calling Esther.

She did need time, but for what, she wasn't sure.

Luke sat on her couch, having postponed his flight until the following day, and he looked like he'd rather be sipping whiskey instead of the seltzer water she'd given him. He hadn't said much of anything since leaving the hotel, and Lexie wanted to crawl into bed and forget today had ever happened.

Instead, she made herself a cup of hot chocolate and joined him in the living room. She sipped and he sipped, and a giant elephant sat in the room with them.

"Did you know about Jason's accident?"

"Yes."

"Was it before or after you brought him home for the holidays?"

"Before, obviously." Luke drained the last of his drink and set the glass on the side table. "You guys didn't get together for another nine years after that." He cut a glance at Lexie. "Don't tell me you had a crush on him when I brought him home."

"No." At least that was the truth. But when she'd seen Jason Burnes, her brother's best friend from college, in that New York City bar, she had thought it might be fate. Foolishness had never burned so hot, and she pressed her lips together as she tried to tame her thoughts.

"So you weren't really friends."

"We were friendly."

"And you did tell everyone about my relationship with him."

Luke met her eye. "Yes." At least he wasn't lying about it anymore.

She wanted to rage at him that his decision had altered the course of her life drastically. She'd hired a bodyguard after that, fallen for a cruel man who knew how to show only his good side in public, and given up her entire existence in her home state.

She wanted to be mad at him, but in the end, she couldn't. Without all of that, she wouldn't be in Getaway Bay, wouldn't be part of the clubs she enjoyed, with the friends she'd managed to find.

"For what it's worth, he's a good bodyguard," Luke said, getting to his feet and returning to the kitchen for more to drink.

The next day, Luke left in the morning and Lexie called Sasha and asked if she could find someone to cover her shift.

"You okay?" her friend asked.

Of course Lexie wasn't okay, but she wasn't going to admit it quite yet. "I'll be fine," she said. "I just want to go sailing today."

"Maybe you need a friend to go with you."

"I'm chartering," she said. And she'd already paid for the whole boat. Her and the three-man crew, a reef, and an afternoon of snorkeling. She loved being under the water, where she couldn't talk to anyone anyway, where she could experience a whole new world.

"Did you break up with Jason?"

"Sort of."

"Sort of?" Sasha repeated. "I didn't know that was possible."

"Sure it is," Lexie said. "Haven't you ever heard of on-again, off-again relationships?"

"So you're off-again? Are you going to wait seven more years to give him a third chance?"

"Very funny." Lexie gazed out the window, partially wishing Steve was there to keep her company. "I'll see you tomorrow." She hung up and went to pack her bag for her afternoon on the reef.

There was nothing quite as cleansing and freeing as snorkeling. She floated on the surface of the water, a world above and a world below. Caught in between. Hovering on the surface. How she'd felt for the last several years but didn't know how to fix.

A school of yellow and black fish swam below her, and relaxation filled her whole body. She kicked around and saw fish, flora, and even an eel, as pointed out to her by Henrietta, the best snorkeling guide in Getaway Bay.

By the time Lexie returned to land, she felt ready to make a decision. She pulled her photo albums out from underneath the television and started leafing through them. In each picture, she found smiles, but her memories conjured up how plastic they were, or what her father had said just before the photo had been snapped.

She didn't like any of these pictures. None of the memories. And her vow to never have alcohol in her life intensified.

She closed the book, wishing she could close that chapter of her life as easily. But there was Jason, trying to elbow his way back in. Literally, as her phone chimed and Jason's name popped up, asking about the car and how he should return it to her.

I can get a shuttle back to Sweet Breeze.

He must be working tonight, so Lexie typed, *Sure, bring it tonight. I'm home,* and sent it She should've known Jason better. Should've known that he wouldn't just leave the keys in the console and head back to work.

Oh, no. Jason rang the doorbell, and Lexie had no choice but to answer it. He wouldn't go away, not until he'd said what he needed to say.

"Hey, Lex."

"Jason."

He held out her keys, and she took them. It seemed impossible that it had only been a week since she'd glared at him near the palm tree and then he'd snuck up on her while she waited at Fisher's private elevator.

"Is there something else you need?" she asked.

The things streaming through his eyes said volumes, but he settled his weight onto one foot and said, "March nineteenth. The accident happened on March nineteenth."

Lexie must've looked as confused as she felt, because he reached up and ran two fingers across her eyebrow, a small smile touching his mouth. "All I ask is you read a little bit about it before you decide to cut me off again." He backed up a step and then another. "You know where to find me."

He turned and went down the steps and then onto the shuttle. Lexie gripped the doorway, the date he'd given her rolling around inside her head. She really didn't like the sight of his back, but she needed to get all her facts laid out before she made a decision that could once again alter her entire course of existence.

SIXTEEN

JASON COULDN'T GO BACK to his place. He wasn't even sure why, only that he didn't want to be there alone, and Steve was still at Jasper's. Tyler had also offered to take the dog, and Jason thought the two men might come to blows over who got to keep Steve.

Finally, Tawny had told Tyler, "Get another dog if you want one, Tyler. It's not like you're too busy," and that had ended things. Jason hadn't been able to stay in the presence of other humans for very long, if only because all of his friends on the island had significant others and they were a constant reminder of how precarious his relationship with Lexie was.

He thanked the shuttle driver and went inside Sweet Breeze, intending to find Sterling and make sure he was okay. He'd gone to the hospital the day before, but they'd patched him up and sent him home. Thankfully, he only had a head wound with a mild concussion—nothing too terribly serious to require him to stay overnight.

Fisher DuPont, the owner of the hotel, had put him up at Sweet Breeze, because Sterling lived alone. He'd been caring for his disabled sister, and Fisher had brought her over too.

He spied Owen leaving the hall that led to his office and detoured toward him. "Hey," he said when Owen saw him. "I can be back on security any time."

"How about in an hour? Rhett quit." Owen looked half-hopeful and half-angry.

"Absolutely." Then Jason wouldn't have to go home. Wouldn't have to wonder if Lexie had looked up the accident and read the reports, the family statements, his own apology and commitment to an alcohol-free life.

He'd kept that promise, and he had no idea what he'd do if his stupid actions and mistakes from almost twenty years ago cost him Lexie. Deep down in his heart, he knew he should've told her when they started dating seven years ago.

He'd apologized for that, given reasons, but was it enough?

"Great." Owen clapped Jason on the back. "Oh, there's Gina. Excuse me."

Jason noticed the hint of interest in Owen's voice and saw the way his whole face lit up. "What's with you and her?" he asked the general manager.

"What? Nothing." Owen pulled at his necktie and strode away, the tips of his ears turning fire engine red, causing Jason to chuckle.

Now that he was working in an hour, he hurried away from the cavernous lobby and down another hall that led to the handful of guest rooms on the first floor. Sterling and his sister were staying in the largest one in the corner, and Jason knocked, calling, "Hey, Sterling. It's Jason."

His fellow valet opened the door a few seconds later, looking completely normal. "Hey, Jason." He smiled, and that was when Jason saw the exhaustion in the man's face. "Come on it. Paulette, Jason's here." Sterling stepped back. "You remember him, right? He helped you into the car once."

Jason entered the room and Sterling closed the door behind them. He passed Jason, who caught sight of the bandages in the man's hair, his throat suddenly narrowing. "How are you feeling?"

Sterling's fingers drifted to the injury. "Tired." He sat on the couch and gave another faint smile. "Come sit down. Paulette has her murder mysteries on, and they're not half-bad."

"I can't stay long," Jason said. "I guess Owen is short-handed with security tonight."

A flash of remorse moved across Sterling's face. "I'm surprised you're not at the valet podium."

"He got Bill to do it."

Bill didn't normally work nights because of his three kids at home. His wife had died the year before, and the man didn't have many people he could get to sleepover with his children. "I think Owen offered to pay his triple the rate." Jason smiled and sat beside Sterling. "He needs the money, so he took it."

They watched the murder mystery in silence for a few

minutes, and then Sterling turned toward Jason. "Thanks for all your help yesterday."

Jason blinked at him, trying to remember the day before. The altercation with Victor and his men felt like it had happened a lifetime ago, not just twenty-four hours ago. "No problem," he said. "I'm sorry you were caught in the middle of it."

"Did you figure out what happened?"

"Most of it," Jason said. He'd hung around the interviews Luke had given, gave his own testimony, and asked the detective in charge to send him anything public he could. So yes, Jason knew as much as anyone else. "Me showing up and pretending to be the valet really threw their getaway driver for a loop. He bolted, so even if we hadn't been in the lobby when they'd burst out, they wouldn't have gotten far."

"You always seem to be in the right place at the right time." Sterling smiled and the action looked a little easier, a little happier.

"If only that were true." Jason chuckled, wondering why he'd had to be in the exact wrong place at the complete wrong time on March nineteenth.

"How's Lexie?" Sterling asked next, and Jason flinched away from the sound of her name.

"She's fine," he said, standing. "Sorry, but I have to get to work. Owen didn't seem like he'd be very happy if I'm late."

"Yeah, go, go." Sterling waved toward the door. "I'll be out to get some dinner in a little bit."

"Make sure you say hi." Jason paused with his hand on

the doorknob and said, "Bye, Paulette. Good to see you again."

The woman's eyes left the television for a minute, and the briefest of moments of recognition entered her expression. She smiled too, and Jason turned to go, knowing that was all he'd get. Still, it was something, and Jason could use every smile thrown his way.

No one else was going to grin at the bulky, beefy security guard who stood next to the registration desk, that was for sure. He kept his arms folded as he watched the comings and goings at Sweet Breeze, the crowd swelling at dinner time and dwindling the later it got.

By midnight, when his shift ended, he'd booked the cheapest room Sweet Breeze offered and when he finally made it to the fourteenth floor, he found a tray of food waiting for him and a handwritten note from Fisher DuPont himself.

No charge for the room, Jason. Stay as long as you want. Thanks for all you've done for my hotel and my friends. ~Fisher

Jason's heart softened and he removed the cloche to find a meatloaf dinner waiting for him. And it was somehow still hot, which made Jason wonder how Fisher knew when and where to orchestra things so seamlessly.

His phone chimed, and he'd just gotten a message from Owen. *Everything okay in the room?*

And Jason knew—it wasn't Fisher who'd done anything except write what Owen had told him to.

Thank you, Owen, he texted back. *Everything's great.*

She'll come around, you know.

"Maybe," Jason said as he typed the letters and sent the

message. But he didn't want to talk about Lexie with Owen, not yet anyway. So he silenced his device and picked up his fork. What he wanted to do right now was eat. So he did.

He stayed at Sweet Breeze for a week, until the walls in the standard room felt like they were closing in on him. He collected his dog from Jasper and Sasha, dozens of questions about The Straw and Lexie and her work schedule burning through his mind. Sasha took forever to find the dog's leash, and when she finally did, she wouldn't relinquish it to Jason immediately.

"She's miserable," she said. "You haven't asked, but I know you want to."

"I don't want to," Jason said, reaching for the leash. He also didn't want to be rude to Sasha, who might be his only lifeline to Lexie. "But I'm sorry to hear she's unhappy."

"She's processing."

"She's very good at that." Jason wound the leash around his hand and looked at the blue canvas coils, his own unhappiness like a scent on the air. Steve seemed to be able to sense it, because he kept nudging Jason's hand with his nose. "Thanks for taking care of Steve this week."

"Oh, he's a sweetheart." Sasha dropped into a crouch. "Aren't you, you sweet thing? Yes you are. Yes you are."

"Are you talking to that dog like a baby again?" Jasper came down the last few steps, grinning at his wife. She straightened and giggled as he pulled her into his side. Jason wanted to bolt and never come back. Frankie,

Jasper's dog, came bounding down the steps too, his tail wagging like he and Steve had become best friends that week.

"Thanks, Jasper," he said, extending his hand to shake Jasper's. "You guys are great."

Jasper shook his hand silently, but the man had keen eyes. Reporter's eyes, and Jason turned toward the door to leave. The last thing he needed was to be sized up. Fleshed out. Judged.

"See you around the island." He stepped outside and Sasha gave a chorus of goodbyes before she closed the door.

Back on his tiny patch of beach, Jason watched Steve sniff something in the sand, dig, and sniff some more. He eventually gave up on whatever he could smell and flopped down, his tongue lolling out of his mouth.

He wore a smile though, and that was more than Jason could do. Had Lexie read the articles yet? It had been seven days since he'd dropped off her car. How long did he have to wait?

As the sun sank into the ocean, Jason told himself to wait a little longer. *Just a little longer....*

By lunchtime the next day, his patience had snapped. He put Steve's leash in his pocket and headed down the beach. The Straw sat around the top curve in the bay, and it took him a good half an hour of walking through squishy sand to get to it. Just enough time to work up a real thirst.

The line in front of the drink stand was non-existent, so it only took one glance and two seconds for him to see that Lexie wasn't working. She often worked afternoons, and perhaps he was too early.

"Raspberry lemonade," he said to Sasha, whose eyebrows zipped up underneath her visor.

"You want lemonade?"

"I mean, I guess." Jason took a few seconds to examine the menu. "I think I'll come back later for a smoothie." He met her eyes, his unspoken question very, very clear.

"Today's not a good day," Sasha said, earning her a look from Maddy.

"What kind of code are you guys speaking?" she asked.

"He's Lexie's boyfriend." Sasha indicated him with the flick of her washcloth.

"Nope." Jason shook his head. "That's the wrong B-word." Though he supposed he couldn't be labeled as her bodyguard either. "When should I come for the smoothie, then?"

Sasha leaned against the counter, a sly smile on her face. "Maybe tomorrow night?"

"Is that a question?"

She seemed to be enjoying this way too much. "Maybe you should come everyday. Keep me in business."

"In that case, give me the Cancer Killer," he said. "That one sounds delicious."

SEVENTEEN

LEXIE PICKED at the plate of food Ira had put in front of her twenty minutes ago. Whenever he hosted the Nine-0 Club at his house, he served a full meal, complete with an appetizer, a soup course, a main dish, and dessert.

He didn't cook, and he wasn't married, but he had the best personal chef on the island. Lexie usually looked forward to his May Day celebration more than another other time of year. But tonight, all she could think about was how everyone had brought someone with them, and her plus-one had been Owen.

Not only that, but Owen had hardly spoken a word to her once he'd discovered Gina Jackson, another new member of the billionaire's club just down the table from them. She hadn't brought a plus-one, and it seemed like Owen was going to play double duty tonight.

Lexie could tell they liked each other from the way Gina kept twirling a curl of her dark hair around her fingers and

Owen had just sprinkled so much pepper on his mashed potatoes they were surely inedible.

Sure enough, he lifted a forkful to his mouth while chuckling over something the beautiful Gina had said and promptly made a choking noise before spitting them back out.

Lexie couldn't help laughing, and that brought every eye at the table to her. "Sorry." She wiped her mouth with a napkin, but all the women in the Beach Club kept their gazes on her. Her fellow Nine-0 Club members went back to their boring conversations about taxes or the stock market, but Lexie couldn't escape Sasha's eyes.

And when she did, she had to look at Gabi. Or Stacey. Or Tawny. Or Esther.

It felt like her worlds had collided completely, and she really didn't like being her by herself. It was an odd feeling, as she'd spent forty years doing things by herself. Making big decisions. Billion-dollar decisions.

And yet, she couldn't decide whether Jason was worth risking her heart. Problem was, she'd already given it to him, which meant she'd been drifting for days and days, hoping a particularly strong wind would come to the island and push her in the right direction.

So far, no luck with the ocean breezes.

She'd stopped dreaming of a hunky, handsome man to come through the line at The Straw. In fact, she barely saw faces anymore. Just heard drink names and calculated the cost, made change, and blended fruits, flowers, and flavorings.

"You haven't eaten anything," Gabi said, turning away from her conversation with Ira.

"Yes, I have. The honey wheat bread was fantastic." She leaned around Gabi and smiled at Ira. "Tell Micah I said so."

Ira blinked at her and then looked at Gabi. "Was that a smile or a grimace?"

"Definitely a grimace." Gabi patted Lexie's hand like she was a toddler. "I think she was trying to smile…."

"*She* is sitting right here." Lexie had never been one to sit around and mope. She didn't have time for such things, and her parents had never allowed it anyway. With her father always at work or drunk, her mother had taken care of everything around the house. Every bill. Every chore. Every child. *Every*thing.

Lexie hadn't known it when she was a child, but as she became a teenager and then realized she'd be taking over the firm, she saw how exhausted her mother really was. And she didn't want that life. She didn't want her father's life either.

She wanted someone she could share her burdens with. Who would support her, and who she could comfort too.

She sighed, and Ira shook his head. "That doesn't sound good. Who does that sigh belong to?"

"Who says it belongs to a person?"

"Come on." He cocked his head and gave her an incredulous look. "I've been in love before."

Gabi swung her head back to him. "You have?"

"Oh, boy," Lexie said. "Now you've done it, Ira." She laughed as the color drained from his face. Thankfully, three waiters entered the dining room with platters of cakes. One of them better be made completely of chocolate or Lexie was never coming back to this club.

Twelve days had passed since she'd seen Jason in the flesh. The man was suspiciously absent from social media, or she could've at least gotten a fix that way. She hadn't looked up the accident, not sure she needed to know all the details.

But she knew better than most that just because something got printed in the paper or on the Internet didn't mean it was true, or even remotely close to accurate. But he'd asked her to read them.

She felt like someone had taken a red-hot poker and slid it across her skin. Over and over, and just as the wounds started to heal, new ones would form.

"You have to do something," she told herself as she fed her stray cats one early morning. It would be June soon, and the beaches would be full. Stacey had a private beach at Aloha Hideaway, and the women had taken to meeting there instead of on the edge of Sweet Breeze's property.

She'd told them all about Jason days ago—nothing too terrible, just that things were complicated and she was working through some difficult truths—and no one had brought him up again. The fact that they didn't want to sit and gossip about her love life, or anyone really, made Lexie really like them.

She knew if she brought up Jason, they'd give her advice. So when the group text came with *Morning Club. Ten o'clock,* from Esther, Lexie decided to put herself on the agenda.

Not that they had an agenda. Everyone didn't even come every time, as evidenced by Gina's response that said, *Running with Owen. Catch you next time.*

Running with Owen.

Lexie had known the general manager at Sweet Breeze for years, and he'd never expressed any interest in a woman —or running, for that matter—until Gina. She wondered how old he was—the gray along his temples and down into his beard certainly said he was older than Gina. Probably by a lot.

Who cares? Lexie thought. Maybe she did because she really wanted to find her own happiness, and it seemed impossible without Jason.

Lexie ran her fingertips along the top of the photo albums she'd moved into her bedroom. She hadn't looked at them again, but when she wasn't looking at the pictures, when she just thought about her childhood and teen years, she'd realized there were some good memories in her mind too.

She showered, which was ridiculous to do before going to the beach, but allowed her the proper mental space to prepare to talk about Jason. Once dressed in her bright blue one-piece and a new pair of flip flops she'd bought at a pop-up shop along the beach, she tapped out a message in the group text.

I want to talk about Jason. Okay?

The messages that came back seemed to appear one on top of the other.

Yes! Sasha.

About time. Stacey.

Absolutely. Esther.

Woot! Tawny.

Lexie smiled at the names of her friends—real friends—and pressed her phone against her heartbeat. It accelerated as her phone buzzed again, foolishly hoping it would somehow be Jason, though he hadn't messaged her once. She thought he might come by The Straw, but he'd stayed stubbornly away. He was very good at disappearing when he wanted to, and she wondered if he was still on the island at all.

Now I want to come! Gina had texted. Another message popped up while Lexie smiled at the first one. *Cutting my run short. Don't start without me.*

Lexie threw her portable charger in her beach bag and collected two bottles of water from the fridge before loading up in her black convertible for a trip down to the beach. She was the second to arrive, finding Esther already set up—and for a while by the looks of the empty potato chip bag.

"Hey," Lexie said, setting her bag down and unfolding her chair. "How long have you been here?"

"An hour?" Esther buried her bright purple toes in the sand. "Can't sleep these days."

"No?" Lexie peered at her friend, but the blonde woman had never really opened up to Lexie. She was Stacey's best friend, and she and Tawny seemed to have a special bond too. Lexie got it. She couldn't be besties with everyone.

Esther shook her head and pushed her sunglasses up on top of her head. "I have news too, but it's the good kind, and I want you to have as much time as you need to talk about

Jason." She wore pure sympathy and compassion in her eyes, and Lexie leaned over and hugged her.

"Thanks, Esther."

"The other girls should be here soon." She settled her sunglasses back in place and slipped lower into her chair. "Want to give me a sneak peek of what you want to talk about?"

The situation couldn't have been more perfect if Lexie had imagined it. "Actually, yes. Can you search for an event? And read about it and be ready to summarize it for the group?"

A line appeared between Esther's eyes. "I guess so."

"It's about Jason, and I haven't been brave enough to read it." Lexie shrugged, her cowardice sounding stupid when she said it out loud.

Esther picked up her phone from where she'd laid it face-down on the arm of her chair. "What am I looking for?"

"There was a car accident," Lexie said, her voice already slipping into a hollow monotone. She cleared her throat and pulled herself out of that empty place. She wanted to feel. It was the only way she'd be able to make a decision.

"March nineteenth. Boston area. Drunk driver. Jason Burnes."

Esther stopped typing as if someone had frozen her thumbs. Her head moved as she looked at Lexie, but Lexie couldn't see her eyes. Thankfully. She nodded, her jaw set. "See why I haven't been able to read it?"

Esther said nothing, only went back to tapping and swiping. She'd obviously found something, because her movements slowed, and she only scrolled on the screen. Lexie looked away from her, her heart pounding in her chest the same way the waves continually drove against the shore.

Stacey arrived, chattering about something at her bed and breakfast. When she realized that neither Lexie or Esther were responding to her, she asked, "What did I miss?"

"Esther has news too," Lexie said.

"You're first," Esther said, looking over at Stacey. "This is going to be intense."

That wasn't what Lexie wanted to hear, and she almost got up and left. But Tawny and Sasha arrived together, right as the clock clicked over to ten.

"Winnie never answered," Sasha said as she got her stuff laid out. "So are we really waiting for Gina?"

"You'd want us to wait for you." Stacey sprayed sunscreen on her arms and shoulders and passed the bottle to Sasha. "In fact, we have waited for you in the past."

Esther handed her phone to Stacey with a single nod, and Stacey, who wasn't wearing sunglasses yet, looked at it. When she looked up, surprise and alarm colored her expression. Glancing from Esther to Lexie, she said, "What is—?"

"Read it," Esther said. "I need help with the summary."

"Summary?" Tawny pulled her streaked hair into a ponytail, her arm muscles prominent. "I have to teach at eleven, so Gina better hurry up."

"Let's give her five more minutes," Esther said. "She needs to be here."

Lexie wondered why Gina needed to be there, but she didn't ask. She just wanted this meeting to be over. Then she'd know what to do.

Gina arrived seven minutes later, sweaty and with only a

towel slung over her shoulder. "You didn't start without me, did you?"

Stacey lowered Esther's phone, her eyes somewhat glazed over. "No, we didn't." She glanced around at the other women. "But if Tawny has to leave at eleven, we better get started."

EIGHTEEN

JASON DEPLANED IN LOS ANGELES, the sun just as wonderful here as it had been in Hawaii. But the air wasn't as crisp, and there were simply too many people.

He'd loved the big city when he'd moved to it from his small town in Virginia. He'd fallen in love with Boston first, where he'd gone to college for a few years. Then Baltimore. Then New York. Then Miami. But nothing compared to Getaway Bay, even though it was quaint and somewhat of a tourist trap. It had a classic American charm he simply hadn't felt anywhere else before.

But he couldn't stay on the island for one more day, walking halfway to The Straw before chickening out and returning home. He'd given Steve to Tyler and said he'd be back when he came back.

He had no idea when that would be. He'd paid the rent on his beach hut for six months, and that didn't run out until the end of August. He had time. Time for what, he didn't know. But he could live cheap—he had before, and California had some great camping.

Maybe he'd simply find himself as he drifted from place to place. He'd enjoyed working with Owen and for Fisher at the hotel. He was good at security, and while it didn't take the brains of a rocket scientist to be a valet, he'd enjoyed that too.

But they weren't careers. They weren't what the type of man Lexie deserved did for a living.

Lexie.

There she was. Always in his thoughts, always influencing his decisions. He liked it as much as it annoyed him.

He bought a notebook on the way out of the airport, intending to write down his thoughts about the interesting people and places he was going to see. He'd always enjoyed writing, even the technical papers in college, where he was trying to make himself fit into the world of finance. A world where, now, he knew he didn't belong.

But he'd been good at newspaper articles and magazine submissions.

"Maybe you could write a book," he told himself as he left the airport, nothing in front of him but the entire continent of North America. And nothing on his back except a pack.

First stop: the beach.

He browsed the postcards and magnets along the boardwalk, selecting something for Sadie Brown. As if summoned by his thoughts of the girl, her mother texted.

How are you? How's Hawaii?

Jason smiled at Lyndsey's message. He didn't keep in

touch with the Browns all that much, but the new article that had just come out had opened the lines of communication again. Jason knew it would die off, same as it had over the years since he'd changed their lives—and his—by getting behind the wheel of that car.

Hawaii's great. Getting some postcards for Sadie.

The Browns had never left Boston, and while their son, Alfie, was older than Jason was at the time of the accident, Sadie was just graduating from high school. Jason had been sending her postcards from his adventures around the world since the accident, and Lyndsey claimed that Sadie had kept them all and looked at them from time to time.

Oh, great doesn't sound good.

Jason frowned at the text, not sure how Lyndsey knew which great was really great and which one wasn't, especially in a text, from across the country.

Great is great, he said, placing the postcards next to the cash register and pulling a couple of dollars out of his wallet. The surf rolled into the beach below, and nothing about being here felt great. The water was different. The atmosphere was different. And he had absolutely no chance of running into Lexie down on that stretch of sand.

His heart twisted. So maybe his great wasn't all that great.

How's Peter? The father of the Brown family was getting ready to retire, and they'd been having a hard time finding a physician to take over the practice he'd built in Boston. Or so Lyndsey kept saying.

Now I know something's wrong. I'm going to call you.

I won't answer, he thumbed out quickly.

Siiiigh. What's going on?

Jason thanked the man and took his postcards, his idea of sitting on the beach and people-watching completely unappealing now. He didn't want to be in California at all. Problem was, he couldn't think of anywhere that would bring him relief.

Jason walked down the sidewalk, not really dressed for the sandy conditions. He contemplated telling Lyndsey about Lexie. She'd always been more of a mother figure to him than his own mother, and he could use some advice.

I met a woman, he typed out. *One I've dated before.*

He'd often wondered if Lydnsey had taken notes of his life, because she came back with *It's not Lexie, is it?*

How did you know that?

Jason, I've only ever heard you talk about one woman, and it was Lexie.

That couldn't be true, but the longer Jason thought about it, the more he realized it was. Plus, Lyndsey would know from his silence that the woman in question was indeed Lexie.

Is it about the article? Lyndsey asked next.

What? No. Jason shook his head, frustrated that Lyndsey would even think that.

Well, then what's going on?

Truthfully, Jason wasn't sure. He'd known Lexie wouldn't handle his past well, but he hadn't imagined it would take her quite this long to come to terms with something that had happened so long ago. That had turned out so well.

In the end, he could sum it up pretty easily. *Her father was an alcoholic.* He stared at the words in the text, wondering if this was his information to share. Her father's behavior did affect him though, it always had.

So he sent the message, expecting Lyndsey to call immediately, despite his declaration that he wouldn't answer.

Surprisingly, she didn't.

Jason, you're not an alcoholic.

Her message was exactly what Jason needed to see, and read, and hear.

Thank you, Lyndsey. Several minutes passed, and Jason started to make his way toward the camping section of the beach. He'd stay one night, and in the morning, see how he felt. Maybe he could bum around the Golden State and be content for a few weeks.

Okay, so shall I talk to this Lexie?

Jason read Lyndsey's message and burst out laughing. *No, I'm good,* he texted.

Because I can. A little heart-to-heart. Set her straight on what kind of man you are.

Warmth filled Jason's soul, and he gazed over the water, wishing he could tell Lexie about this surrogate family that he'd come to find in the strangest way.

It'll work out, Lyndsey said next.

Jason read those words again and again, hoping with everything inside him that she was right. But the ocean between him and Lexie felt as metaphorical as it was currently physical.

NINETEEN

"OKAY, so I'm going to start at the beginning," Lexie said. "It'll be fast, I promise." She exchanged a glance with Stacey, who wore the worry right on her face. Lexie didn't like that, but she couldn't stop now.

"I grew up with an alcoholic father. Jason and I dated in New York for about a year, seven years ago. When the market crashed, my company almost went under. My brother sold Jason to the press, and he lost his life in the city." She had too, but that wasn't an important detail for them.

"Fast forward to now, and we started about where we left off seven years ago, what?" She looked at Sasha. "A few weeks ago. Stuff happened, and we broke up."

"What stuff?" Gina asked.

Lexie nodded at Esther, who glanced at her phone though the screen was blank. "When he was twenty-one-years-old, Jason got in a car accident with a family of four. He was drunk."

Every eye pinged back to Lexie. "That happened, but I didn't know about it until recently. He didn't tell me that when we dated in New York, and from the time I was fourteen, I'd vowed I would never drink and neither would anyone I dated."

"Jason pled guilty," Stacey said. "The family didn't want his life ruined. No one was killed. I think that article said the worst injury was a broken leg. The dad."

"The mother pleaded for the judge to send Jason to rehab and community service and a treatment program instead of jail." Esther surveyed the group of women, who all seemed like this was the best story they'd heard in a long time. Lexie had heard part of it already, but she still found it fascinating. "The judge complied."

"Jason went into a six-month treatment program which included complete sobriety. Counseling. Community service." Stacey looked right at Lexie and added, "He's been sober since. He meets with an Alcoholics Anonymous counselor every year, on March nineteenth to declare it."

Lexie had not known that and her wounded heart started whispering about how Jason could fit into her life. That he was a good guy. Kind. Hard-working. He wasn't a drunk.

He wasn't her father.

"The family mails him cards and letters every year, on the anniversary of the accident." Esther sniffled, and Lexie wondered why she wasn't crying. Was she really that cold? Blind? Something else?

No one else seemed weepy, though, and Stacey took an

extra moment to study Esther before she said, "Jason sends them gifts and cards too. It's like they became a family. They forgave him, and instead of condemning him, incorporated him into their lives."

Lexie startled. A family. Jason had always wanted a tight-knit family.

"It's really quite touching," Esther said. "I'll forward you guys the article. It was just written this past March."

"Wait," Lexie blurted, the first word she'd said. "This past March? Like six weeks ago?"

"That's right."

"Jason was here, in Getaway Bay, in March."

Sasha looked at her. "So?"

"Did he give quotes in the article?" Lexie suddenly wished she'd read it.

"Yes," Esther wiped her eyes. "I'm such a baby. I don't know what's wrong with me."

Stacey put her hand on Esther's. "In the piece, he says they're more like his family than his actual family, and he's so grateful they gave him a second chance." She pinned a look on Lexie, who couldn't hold still.

"This would technically be our third chance," Lexie said weakly.

"Take it," Sasha said immediately.

Tawny nodded, as did Gina. But frustration filled Lexie. "It's not that easy, you guys."

"No?" Stacey folded her arms and leaned back in her chair. "I flew to Michigan to get Fisher back."

"I went to Switzerland."

Lexie knew that, as she'd taken over The Straw so Sasha could go to Jasper, get him back, make things right.

"So what?" she asked, throwing up her arms. "I just march over to his beach house and say…what? What do I say?"

"That an accident—an accident—*from twenty years* ago doesn't matter." Gina shrugged, like it was no big deal. Like a *lifetime* of Lexie's emotions and experiences meant nothing. "Ask him if he drinks. Believe what he says."

"That sounds good, actually," Tawny said, twisting off the cap of her water bottle.

"I don't know." Lexie wrung her hands, her mind racing as fast as her heart.

"It's simple," Stacey said. "Do you love him?"

"I—"

"Just yes or no." Stacey leaned forward and put her elbows on her knees. "Don't think. Just—do you love him?"

"Yes," Lexie whispered.

"Then fix this." Esther swept her phone into her beach bag as a whistle rent the air, catching the attention of all the women.

"Oh, it's Tyler. He's early. My class doesn't start for another twenty minutes." Tawny shaded her eyes though she wore a pair of sunglasses and stood up. "Um, guys? Tyler's coming this way, and he has *two* dogs."

Lexie practically knocked her chair over she stood so fast. "Two dogs?" She couldn't even find Tyler, but she did see his big golden retriever. The second dog seemed to be playing hide-and-seek really well.

"I think I'm going to be sick," Esther said, standing too and taking a few steps away.

Lexie turned toward the group, her nerves firing on all cylinders. "Is it Steve?"

"I don't know," Tawny said. "I told him to get another dog. Maybe he did."

Esther returned to the semi-circle, her nausea apparently gone. "Guys, real quick, before Tyler gets here and Tawny has to leave."

Everyone looked at her, and Lexie thought she already knew Esther's news. "First, I think Lexie should go find Jason and talk to him. Isn't everything better when we talk to our men?"

Stacey gave a half-shrug and nodded. "Let's vote. Who thinks Lexie should get back together with Jason?"

Every hand went up. "Yeah, but this isn't junior high and we're voting on what to do on Friday night," Lexie said.

"It's your choice," Esther said, laying a hand on Lexie's arm. "But he's a good guy. Read the articles. You'll see."

"He's ten seconds out," Tawny said. "Sorry, guys."

"It's fine," Esther said. "My news is quick. I'm pregnant."

Lexie grinned, her guess at Esther's news right on the bullseye. Shrieking and hugging happened, and Stacey and Tawny both wiped their eyes as the chatter intensified. Tyler must've sensed an overload of estrogen, because he paused out of earshot, a questioning look on his face.

Then his dog dropped the Frisbee at his feet, and he picked it up and sent it soaring again. And the second dog that went tearing after it was Steve.

Lexie hugged Esther and said, "Congratulations, Esther.

You'll be a fantastic mom," and edged away from the Beach Club.

"Tyler." She tucked her hands in her back pockets. "Have you seen Jason?"

Tyler just blinked at her. "I don't know."

"You don't know if you've seen Jason?"

Tyler sighed and ran his hand through his long, surfer hair. "I don't know if he wants you to know."

"Know what?" Lexie exchanged a glance with Tawny as she arrived and stood at Lexie's side.

"How long are we keeping Steve?" she asked as Lazy Bones brought the Frisbee back again. Steve didn't seem to have a clue what to do with the Frisbee, but he seemed overjoyed to be chasing it.

Tyler sent them away again and met his wife's eyes. "Indefinitely. Jason gave him to me."

Lexie's heart dropped to the sand and rebounded to the top of her skull. "What?" she managed to rasp.

"What do you mean he gave you Steve?" Tawny put her hands on her hips, her cut and tied shirt showing her neon lemon bra top underneath. "Where is he?"

Yes, Lexie wanted to know that too, and she searched Tyler's face for any hints.

"I don't know," Tyler said for the third time. It was really starting to ignite Lexie's anger. "He asked if I wanted Steve, because he was leaving the island."

Leaving the island.

Lexie stumbled back a step as if Tyler's words had pushed her. Tawny grabbed onto her hand and steadied her. "Tyler," she said in a calm, even voice. "He didn't tell you *anything*? Where he was going? What flight he was on? *Any*thing?"

"His first stop was in LA," Tyler said, ducking his chin and dropping his eyes to the Frisbee Lazy Bones had just retrieved. "Sorry, Lex. I didn't know what was going on with you guys, and every time I tried to talk to him about it, he shut me down."

"He's a private guy," Lexie said, dumbfounded that she was defending him. But of course she was. She was in love with him. Maybe that was all she had to do. Text him that she loved him and ask him where he was.

Hope lifted her spirits and clogged her throat.

"When did he leave?" Tawny asked.

"Yesterday."

The word punched her in the gut, but Lexie fought against the panic. "Tawny, I have to go. Can you—I'll ask Sasha. I know you have to get to work."

"Keep us updated!" Tawny called after her, and Lexie waved to indicate she'd heard. She arranged with Sasha to get her stuff off the beach, because Lexie couldn't spare even another minute.

I love you, she typed out. *And Tyler said you left the island yesterday? Where are you? I'll come to you. Please, Jason.*

She stared at the words, almost tripping in the sand as she walked back to her car. She didn't care that she sounded desperate. That she'd told him she loved him for the first time in a text. She was desperate and she did love him.

She mashed her thumb on send and headed for the airport. It didn't matter that she wore a swimming suit and a pair of black shorts. She had a credit card—and sheer determination to find Jason, ask him the tough questions, and make things right between them.

Because she loved him. Could he love her too? After her radio silence and harsh judgment?

She sure hoped so, but in all the time it took to get to the airport, buy a ticket, and board the first flight across the ocean to Los Angeles, he still hadn't responded to her text.

TWENTY

BY THE TIME Jason's plane touched down, he wanted to crawl into bed and not get out for a good long while. He'd gotten the last seat on the plane, and it was in the very back row. So he stayed in his seat, his eyes closed, as the rest of the people gathered carry-ons, packed up laptops and headphones, and inched their way toward the exit.

His phone chimed, but he ignored it. Probably Tyler trying to get him to talk about Lexie again. Or worse, Lyndsey offering to talk to Lexie again.

He didn't need either item in his life at the moment, as his patience was already razor thin and his exhaustion was at its pinnacle.

If he could just get back to his beach house, he'd be able to figure out what to do. He thought he could replace Getaway Bay with another beach, but he'd been wrong. Fill his life with other people besides Lexie, but that was the worst mistake of all.

So he'd camped on the beach and gotten on the first flight back to Hawaii. At the beach hut, the six-hundred square feet felt perfect, and he dropped his backpack on the floor by the front door and moved to the back, wishing he could call in his Brittany spaniel and curl up with the dog to sleep away his foul mood.

He plugged in his phone, the green flashing light mocking him. He swiped the phone open and sucked in a tight breath when he saw Lexie's name on his screen.

"She texted me." His voice held a measure of awe, and he immediately started calculating how long it had taken him to get off the plane, get home, and get his act together to check his phone.

Probably thirty minutes. At least.

I love you. And Tyler said you left the island yesterday? Where are you? I'll come to you. Please, Jason.

Jason read the words again, and then again.

I love you.

I love you?

Jason gave his head a little shake and started typing. *I'm at home. Where are you?* He sent the message, everything in him hoping she'd say, *Just down the beach at The Straw. Come get a drink!*

But she didn't respond at all.

He gripped his phone for several long minutes, his desperation, exhaustion, and impatience growing more and more intense by the second.

He didn't understand. She'd texted him thirty minutes ago. She couldn't have gotten too busy.

"Maybe there's a rush," he said. "Or she could be in a

meeting. She'll text back." He didn't bother to get the Murphy bed out but simply lay down on the couch, his phone tucked right against his chest.

He woke—hours later if the darkness in the sky was any indication—when his phone rang. Blinking, he tried to figure out what time it was, where he was, who was calling.

Seeing Lexie's name, he scrambled to a sitting position and swiped the call on. "Lex," he said, his voice a bit rusty from sleep.

"You're at home?"

"Yes." He got up and walked to the front door as if she'd be waiting outside. "Where are you?"

She exhaled, her frustration obvious, but followed it with a light laugh. "Well, I'm in LA."

"LA?"

"Tyler said you flew to LA."

He could imagine her wiping her hair off her face and glancing around, trying to figure out what to do. He opened his front door, still half-hoping he'd see her there. He didn't.

"I did, yeah," he said, feeling like a fool. "I thought... well, it doesn't really matter what I thought. It was a stupid thought, and I got on a plane home this morning."

"I got on a plane to LA at noon," she said.

"And with the time difference...." Jason chuckled, his laughter growing at the irony of the situation. Once he sobered, he said, "Lex, I got your text."

"Oh."

"I love you too."

A sigh came through the line, and Jason hated that there

were thousands of miles of ocean separating them. "I'll get on the first flight back."

"Won't be until tomorrow," he said.

"Are you sure?"

"Seemed that way to me."

"I'll do the best I can."

Jason stepped onto the front porch and took a deep breath of the island air. He couldn't believe he thought he could leave Getaway Bay and be happy. "It's so good to hear your voice," he said. "I can't…I mean, what changed your mind?"

Had she read the articles?

"We can talk about it when I get there. You sound tired."

"I am tired."

"So you go back to sleep, and I'll call you when I'm back on the island."

"All right, sweetheart." He leaned against the pillar. "Love you, Lex."

And the most magical words on the planet were "Love you too, Jason."

Dawn found Jason lying in the hammock in his back yard, listening to the waves roll against the bay. The only thing that could've made the morning better was Steve lying near his head, his somewhat obnoxious panting harmonizing with the waves.

Or Lexie.

Yes, Lexie would've made this dawn absolutely beautiful.

He became aware of someone walking toward him, but it was still quite dark and he couldn't see who it was.

He sat up, the wires on the hammock squeaking, and someone said, "Jason?"

"Lexie." He launched himself out of the hammock, the sound of her voice like a balm to his weary soul. He strode toward her, a darker silhouette on the lightening horizon, and he cupped her face in his hands, his eyes searching hers.

"Jason."

There was a lot to say, many things to work through, but Jason never was one to beat around the bush. He dipped his head and kissed her, this woman who he'd loved for so, so long.

She kissed him back, matching his passion stroke for stroke, until finally she leaned her forehead against his. "I can't believe I was flying to Los Angeles while you were on a plane back here." She giggled and wrapped her arms around him. "We must've crossed paths at forty thousand feet."

He chuckled and ran his lips along her neck. "Probably. No cell service that high, right?"

"Right."

He kissed her again but pulled back swiftly. "Hey, how did you get here so fast?" Even with the time difference, he hadn't expected her until much later in the day.

"Jason, I'm a billionaire. I didn't wait for the next commercial flight."

He gazed at her, struck by her beauty, her resourcefulness, her wit. "Don't tell me you bought a jet."

"Just a one-time use," she said. "And I paid a crew to

leave immediately. It was quite an expensive flight." She pressed into him and smiled. "But totally worth it."

Jason had spent so long wondering if anyone could love him, and then Lyndsey Brown had come into his life. She'd loved him, even though he'd done something unspeakable to her and her family.

And now Lexie stood in front of him, making him feel worthy of being loved.

"Did you read the articles?"

"Only one."

"Which one?"

"The one that just came out a few weeks ago."

He'd been hoping she'd see that one. Lyndsey and Peter had said such nice things about him. He almost believed they were true, and now with Lexie looking at him with such adoration in her expression, he thought what the Browns had been telling him for years might actually be true.

"It's in the past," she said. "But I do need to ask you one thing, and I hope it doesn't offend you."

"I already know what it is." At least he thought he did. "But go ahead."

She stepped out of his arms, the golden light from the sun starting to halo her. She was positively radiant, despite being on a plane for much of the last eighteen hours, despite the way she pressed her fingertips together and swallowed hard.

"When's the last time you had a drink of alcohol?"

"March nineteenth, seventeen years ago."

Lexie nodded, her jaw set. "I believe you. You're an amazing man, Jason."

"I am not."

"Not many men could overcome what you have."

"I'm a drifter. No goals. No idea what I'm doing with my life, and I'm almost forty years old."

She grinned at him, though he wasn't sure what she was so happy about. "Just like the rest of us, then."

He scoffed. "Come on, Lex. You're the CEO of a huge financial firm."

"I work part-time at a drink stand on the beach."

"But you don't have to."

"I'm less lonely when I do."

"Sweetheart." He drew her close again, tucking her right against his heart. "I'm hoping I can help with that too."

"I'm sure you can." Her eyes sparkled with inner light, with happiness, with love.

Jason touched the tip of his nose to hers. "I love you, Lexie. Even if you work part-time at a drink stand."

"And I love you, Jason, even if you are a drifter. It's kind of romantic."

Jason tipped his head back and laughed, his emotions such a different kettle of fish from yesterday morning. He'd only been this happy once before—when he was Lexie's secret boyfriend in New York.

She traced her fingers down the side of his face, and he sobered long enough to kiss her again.

TWENTY-ONE

LEXIE DOZED in Jason's arms, her arms wrapped around him, never wanting to let go. He seemed to feel the same way, because he kept the hammock swaying slightly and didn't complain when the temperature reached unbearable levels.

So snuggled in to his side and said, "Should we go inside? I'm boiling."

"Mm." But Jason didn't move, so peaceful and content with their current situation.

Lexie pushed herself up, using the hard planes of his chest to balance. "Do you have any ice cream in your freezer?"

"Nope." He stroked his fingers down her back.

"Let's go get some." She leaned over him, smiling when he finally looked at her instead of the ocean. "Please?"

Jason grinned at her and kissed her. Lexie wondered how

on earth she'd thought she could live without him. Because what she'd been doing for the past two weeks certainly hadn't been living.

He held her face in his hands, slowing their kiss until he finally broke their connection. "Lex, how are you feeling about kids? We talked about it so long ago, and I'm just…wondering."

Lexi put her legs over the side of the hammock and watched the waves Jason seemed so enamored with. "I am forty," she said. "So if we wanted kids, we'd probably need to get started on that right away."

"I don't have a problem with that." He sat up next to her and took her hand in his. "Means you're going to want to get married like, tomorrow, right?"

Panic filled Lexie and she whipped her attention to him. "Tomorrow?" She laughed, sure he was kidding. But he didn't even smile. A playful glint twinkled in his eye.

"So next week," he said.

Lexie searched his gaze, trying to decide if he really wanted to get married next week. "Don't you want to invite your parents?"

His jaw clenched, and he focused back on the water. Steve looked up at him as if the dog could sense Jason's anxiety. Lexie certainly could. The animal whined, and Jason reached down and gave him a little pat.

"You know what, Lex? I don't want to invite them." He faced her, his expression softening. "I just want you and me, and our friends. The people who love us and have been involved in our lives. My parents don't fit into any of those categories."

Lexie accepted his answer and nodded. "What about Luke?"

"Luke is welcome," Jason said coolly. "It was never me that had the problem, Lex. He's so much like your father, though. He won't approve."

Lexie already knew that and she didn't care. "My brother doesn't have the power to take things from me I've worked my whole life to have."

"So two weeks?"

She giggled and nudged him with her elbow. "I still want to invite my brothers. I should probably call them and see what the company schedule is like."

Jason didn't respond, and Lexie asked, "What?"

"It's our wedding," he said. "I don't want Luke to dictate when we'll celebrate our anniversary for the next fifty years."

Fifty years. The words rang in Lexie's ears, in Jason's deep voice, and she sure liked the sound of them. She stood up and stretched, feeling hot and sweaty and yet downright wonderful.

"Okay, let me get my calendar open." She plucked her phone from her purse and swiped open an app. "Sasha only schedules me two weeks out, so—"

"Are we going to go on a honeymoon?" Jason stood too and stretched. "I'd like to go on an Alaskan cruise."

"You want to go from Hawaii to Alaska?"

Jason caught her around the waist. "Yes, ma'am. The two states not everyone has visited. We'd be like world travelers."

"Hate to break it to you, but Hawaii is one of the most

popular vacation destinations." She laughed as he grinned down at her.

"I can't pay for it," he said. "But maybe you'd need a bodyguard to accompany you on a dangerous, deadly Alaskan cruise?"

Lexie laughed and kissed him, happier than she'd ever been.

"Three weeks?" Jason murmured, his lips skating across her jaw to her ear.

Five weeks later, Lexie stood in Stacey's private suite, fiddling with the hem of her veil. It curled strangely and steaming hadn't been able to straighten it.

"It's fine," Sasha said, swatting Lexie's hand away. "I can't believe you're getting married today." She hugged Lexie for about the tenth time that day and beamed at her. "Now Esther's ready to put the flowers in, so you won't be able to play around with it anymore."

"I'm not playing around with it." She brushed her fingers against it. She wore an orange T-shirt and a pair of cutoffs with the veil, which was a little strange. But the dress would be the last thing she put on, only a few moments before she walked from Aloha Hideaway to the altar in the gardens, where she'd be married.

After she and Jason had picked a date, she'd called Luke and Bruce, told them when it would be and that she'd love to have them there while she tied the knot. They'd both come, and though her brother had barely looked away from his phone, he was here.

No one from Jason's family had come, and he'd insisted that he was fine, that he'd done exactly what he wanted to do—and all he wanted was to marry Lexie.

Lexie had then gone to her Women's Beach Club and freaked out about planning a wedding in five weeks. Her friends had rallied around her, as four of them had actually exchanged nuptials quite recently.

Dividing up the list, the five women had managed to get the venue, hire someone to do the cake, and go dress shopping. Lexie and Jason got pictures taken, and announcements sent, and everything was going without a hitch.

Esther pinned hibiscus flowers in her hair, along with white lilies, until she was wearing the most beautiful flower crown, her veil flowing out of it as if the two pieces were really one.

"Almost done," Esther said at the same time Sasha said, "Hurry up, Esther. The ceremony begins in fifteen minutes, and we still have to do the dress."

The dress was quite complicated, but it was absolutely perfect and everything Lexie had pictured herself getting married in.

"Done." Esther stood and moved back a few steps, studying her handiwork. Her face bloomed into a smile. "Beautiful."

"Dress, dress, dress," Sasha said, latching onto Lexie like she couldn't walk on her own now that the flowers were in her hair.

Lexie stepped out of her clothes and let Sasha shimmy the dress up and over her hips. Lexie held the dress in place over her chest as Esther and Sasha started to button her into it.

The door opened, and Stacey came in. "Almost ready?"

"Almost," Sasha said over her shoulder.

"Can Lexie have a guest?"

Lexie turned from the window, wondering who would be coming to see her now. "Who is it?"

Stacey stepped further into the room, pressing the door open a bit more and leaving room for a tall, beautiful woman to enter. She wore love in her expression, but Lexie had no idea who she was.

"Oh, you must be Jason's Lexie." She opened her arms wide like Lexie would step into her embrace and soak up her warmth. Instead, she looked at Stacey, and then Esther.

"I'm Lyndsey Brown," she said as if that would solve everything.

Stacey beamed and nodded like she knew who Lyndsey Brown was.

"I'm sorry…." Lexie said, trying to communicate telepathically with Stacey.

Sasha stepped in front of Lexie, her buttoning abandoned. "Lyndsey Brown? Oh, you're the woman from the accident." She spun back to Lexie. "She was the mom in Jason's car accident." Sasha looked so earnest, so alive, and like this woman's appearance at Lexie's wedding was a godsend.

But Lexie was still confused. Lyndsey came closer, the wisdom in her eyes so much like Lexie's mom that she barely flinched when the woman took over Sasha's job and started buttoning. "What a beautiful dress. No wonder Jason's been in love with you for so long." She looked perfectly at ease behind Lexie, and she kept trying to catch the woman's eye in the mirror.

"We've kept in touch over the years," Lyndsey said, finally looking up. "You're exactly the kind of woman I always pictured him with."

Lexie was still having a hard time processing the situation. But she managed to ask, "Did he invite you to the wedding?"

"Yes." Lyndsey smiled and finished the buttons before running her fingers down the tiny loops that had already been done. "Jason's like family to us."

Lexie turned toward her. "Family?"

Lyndsey beamed at her, tears shining in her eyes. "My daughter can't wait to meet you." She gave Lexie's shoulders a hug, and added, "I can tell I'm slowing things down. I just wanted to introduce myself and say how happy we are for you and Jason."

She nodded to the other women in the bride's room on her way out, and Stacey went with her saying, "Four minutes, Lex," before she closed the door.

Lexie stared at the wood and then switched her gaze to Sasha, who shrugged.

"Jason didn't tell you?" Esther asked.

"He said he'd invited a few important people." Lexie faced herself, glad he had someone here who obviously loved him.

"Well, you're the most important person now." Sasha

swept the shoes out of the box and said, "Step in. Then we'll go."

Lexie slipped into her shoes, accepted the bouquet from Esther, and started toward the garden to get married. It was a small affair, with exactly who Jason wanted in attendance—their friends, family, and people they loved.

Stacey had designed the garden to host weddings, and the wedding march piped through the speakers somewhere in the trees overhead. Her father wasn't there to walk her down the aisle, but she laced her arm through Jasper's and waited while the rest of the wedding party went down the aisle ahead of her.

Finally everyone was in position and Jasper said, "You ready for this, Lex?"

Her eyes locked onto Jason, down at the altar. "So ready."

When Jasper passed her to Jason, he swept his arm around her and said, "You're stunning," before facing the minister. His weathered face smiled back at them, and Lexie tried to pay attention to what he said, she honestly did.

But she really just wanted to be pronounced Jason's wife, so she could kiss him and be his forever.

Finally, the minister said, "I now pronounce you man and wife," and "You may kiss your bride."

Jason looked at her with love, desire, and just enough tease that Lexie said, "Jason," in a warning voice.

He wrapped both arms around her and dipped her back, pausing just before kissing her to the whoops and applause of their guests. When they straightened, Jason turned toward everyone and lifted their joined hands.

The people in the front row came forward to give hugs, and it was Lyndsey and her family, and Lexie took one look at Jason and saw that yes, these people were his family.

And Lexie felt warm from head to toe. She accepted hugs from the Brown family, her brothers, her billionaire friends, and her Women's Beach Club before she and Jason escaped the festivities.

"We have to go back out in a few minutes," he said. "Dinner. Dancing." But he looked at her with all the desire a man should look at his new wife.

"Don't mess up my hair," she said. "Esther will be so mad." She squealed as Jason growled and swept her into his arms.

"I love you," he said, his hands hot along her waist as his fingers played with one of the buttons on the back of her dress.

"And I love you." She traced her fingertips down the side of his face. "I can't wait to get to know the Browns the way you do."

"You'll love them."

"They love you."

"Thank you for taking a third chance on me," he whispered just before kissing her, and Lexie felt like she was the one who had been given everything in the world, including the love of this good man.

Read on for a sneak peek of the first chapter of **SWEET**

BREEZE RESORT, the next book in the Getaway Bay Resort series.

SNEAK PEEK! SWEET BREEZE RESORT CHAPTER ONE

GINA JACKSON WHISTLED while she worked in the corner of the suite, her measuring tape making a metallic crinkling sound as she tried to get it all the way against the wall.

She and Owen Church, the general manager here at Sweet Breeze, had talked about taking these boring, blah closets into something spectacular for the longer-stay guests at the premier hotel and resort in Getaway Bay.

Gina Jackson could still taste the dill cream cheese she'd eaten on her bagel over an hour ago. She really needed a mint—and for her blasted tape measure to stop acting all wonky.

The metallic crinkling sound grated against her nerves as she shook the end of it into the corner. The closets at Sweet Breeze Resort and Hotel were nothing like any she'd worked on before. They were almost like rooms of their own, and while Gina had taken closet organization into a billion-dollar business, her nerves squirmed at the thought of messing up this job.

Thus, her bagel breakfast with the boss over this project at Sweet Breeze, Owen Church. *Boss* ran through her mind. She and Owen were definitely working together, though he wasn't really her boss. He was the general manager at the hotel, and his opinion was all that mattered. Gina had noticed that the owner of the hotel—Fisher DuPont—didn't call nearly as many shots as Owen did.

She'd marveled at that for a while, as she finished a couple of other jobs on the island and contemplated not returning to the mainland at all.

She'd seen Owen and Fisher together, felt their energy, and envied the complete trust between them. She used to have a partner like that, but the lure of money and power had been too great, and the betrayal coursing through Gina definitely still stung.

The tape measure simply wouldn't cooperate today, and she wasn't sure the ideas she'd discussed with Owen while he smeared strawberry cream cheese over a cinnamon raisin bagel would even work.

She'd never understand his weird food combinations, and they'd been sharing a lot of meals together lately. Most in his office, or here at the hotel after their morning run.

Gina couldn't seem to get Owen out of her mind, not even long enough to measure a simple space, something she could normally do with just the naked eye.

She sighed, determined not to let the handsome man distract her from the job, and not to let the job—a huge, multi-million dollar job that could establish her in the hotel industry— consume her very existence.

With her foot, she stomped the end of the measuring device into the carpet and finally pulled the tape taught. "Seventeen feet, two inches," she muttered to herself. And that was just the depth of this closet. The width had to be easily twice that.

Fisher had designed the hotel to be the best of its kind, but he hadn't truly thought of those who might want a long-term stay. As more and more businessmen and women came to Getaway Bay, he'd realized a need for such a suite.

Well, Gina suspected it was Owen who'd noticed the need, run it all by Fisher, and then started remodeling their nicer suites into long-term stay apartments.

Gina had been contracted to take some of the existing space and make it into a closet. With the smell of fresh paint from the new kitchen area just around the corner, she once again pushed against the anxiety that she couldn't do this job. That it was too big for her. That her normal master bedroom closet in a single-family home in Dallas simply hadn't provided her the experience she needed for a job of this magnitude, on this scale.

Sure, she'd done the five rooms at the bed and breakfast down the beach. The owner had been thrilled, but they were basically bedrooms with normal sized closets Gina had simply taken up a notch.

But Fisher's wife had been so complimentary that this job at Sweet Breeze had basically fallen into Gina's lap. She couldn't say no, even if she felt leagues out of her, well, league.

She took a few more measurements and consulted her catalog for systems that might fit. It would be ultra-expensive to have a custom-built organization system, but she couldn't find anything that seemed like it would work. Everything in her catalog was too small for a space like this.

Sighing, she left the bedroom and went into the main living area, which was in a state of construction. "Maybe the closet doesn't need to be that big," she said to the drop cloth protecting the tile floor in the kitchen area. The appliances still had plastic on them, and she had to be out of the room in an hour so the painters could finish.

Then it was just loading the room with the furniture, the new linens, drapes, accessories—oh, and her closeting system.

Desperation pushed against her tongue, but she swallowed it back. She would not panic. She could do it.

"You can do this," she said aloud and went back into the bedroom. This suite sat in the corner on the fifth floor. Owen wanted two dozen long-term stay apartments, some one-bedroom suites like the one where Gina stood now, and some with two bedrooms. She'd been through those, but she hadn't been able to take measurements or spend much time in the room, as it had been in the middle of the demolition process to turn the suite into an apartment.

"Maybe the closet is just too big," she said to the stark room, something Owen had said that morning. They'd gone over a few designs, and he'd liked them all. She'd expressed her concerns over the size, the measurements, and making sure it looked high-end like he wanted, but remained functional—her trademark.

Everyone should have a closet that works for them. That was her company motto, one she'd written herself for Classy Closets, and that she stuck to on every job she took.

After all, it made no sense to hire a professional organizer and licensed interior designer to get something that wasn't even usable.

She stepped around the scaffolding in the room the painters used and shook out her measuring tape again. "There could be a separate dressing area here," she said, thinking out loud. "It would shave off a few feet, and give me access to the twelve-foot systems."

Gina turned in a slow circle, imagining the shelving, the hanging ranks, the spot the iron would go—with a fold-out board that disappeared seamlessly into the wall. She saw the island in the middle, an easy spot for travelers to put their bags and unpack for their stay. Extra towels, robes, and linens could go in the cupboards on the island so guests wouldn't have to call and wait—or bother housekeeping—for basic needs.

She envisioned a shoe rack down the wall, as well as a high hanging rack for suits and formal dresses. Then, through the door, the dressing area, with full-length mirrors on two walls.

"That's it," she said. "That's what we need in here." Excitement coursed through her that she'd solved this problem. Now, she just needed to talk to Owen, because this wasn't an easy fix for him. She was proposing more construction, more expenses with another door, mirrors, and that extra rack.

Still, she could see the closet in her mind, and it was

exactly what this suite needed. She wasn't the best salesperson on the planet, but she'd draw the blueprint for him and see what he said.

Owen loved blueprints, and Gina grinned to herself as she twisted to go find him. She'd gotten turned around in the room as the closet came to life inside her mind, and she stubbed her toe against the scaffolding.

"How's it going?"

Gina yelped, first in pain, and then fright at the deep male voice. She hopped on her good foot, but that didn't help her keep her balance.

She knew she was going down—and right in front of those dark, deep, dreamy eyes of Owen's—before she did. She frantically reached for the scaffolding—anything to anchor herself—though her brain screamed at her that it was a bad idea. The last thing she needed was to pull the metal structure down on top of her.

She missed anyway, blast her poor coordination. The beautiful closet disappeared from her mind as she flopped backward, Owen's voice somewhere beyond her going, "Gina."

Everything happened so fast, and while Gina didn't consider herself old by any means, her thirty-six-year-old body protested at the hardness of the floor against her tailbone, shoulders, and head.

Owen appeared in her vision. "Are you okay? I didn't mean to startle you." He wore a look of pure panic, sorrow, and compassion.

All Gina could do was stare into those eyes that followed her into her dreams and shake her head.

"You're not okay?" His gaze sharpened and he pulled out his phone. One tap. Two swipes, and he said, "Jillian, it's Owen. I need medical on the fifth floor, suite 512."

Gina kept shaking her head. "I'm okay."

Owen looked very doubtful and kept his phone at his ear. "Gina Jackson fell." He reached out with his free hand and swept his fingers across her face, letting them linger in her hair.

She couldn't read his expression at all, but he jolted away from her as if he'd been shocked and sat back on his heels. "She's talking…five minutes. Thank you, Jillian."

He hung up and hovered over her again. "Someone is coming, Gina. Five minutes."

As if she hadn't heard him already. "I'm fine," she said again, this time pushing herself into a seated position. At least all her running and beach yoga had made it possible for her to do such a thing. She'd taken up exercise after Ian, the partner who'd betrayed her, had left Classy Closets, taking so much of Gina and her company with him that she hardly recognized herself anymore.

He certainly wouldn't recognize her now, not fifty pounds lighter, with the dark hair she got from a bottle, and more success than she'd achieved previously, simply by doing everything herself. No partners.

Owen touched her face again, drawing Gina back to this embarrassing moment. "Did you hit your head?"

Gina reached up and touched the back of her head, where a lump was forming. "Yeah. Right here."

Owen's fingers probed through her hair gently, sending

sparks down her spine and fire through her blood. "Ah, yes. It's not too big though."

Maybe if she said her back hurt, he'd rub it. Gina gazed at him, wondering at the powerful current between them. She'd always found him handsome. Kind. Dedicated. Loyal. And he was probably the only person on the planet who worked more than she did.

"I just came to see how things were going," he said, letting his fingers linger in her hair.

She leaned into his touch, her eyes drifting halfway closed. Could he feel this energy between them? What if she was the only one who felt like she was falling toward an unknown source of gravity, with no way to catch herself? "I had an idea."

"I have one too." His voice rumbled through Gina, and she barely had time to open her eyes before his lips touched hers.

A gasp pulled through her whole body, and suddenly nothing hurt anymore.

Read SWEET BREEZE RESORT today. You'll get to see a workplace romance between a single dad and a new billionaire on the island!

BOOKS IN THE GETAWAY BAY RESORT ROMANCE SERIES

Aloha Hideaway Inn (Book 1): Can Stacey and the Aloha Hideaway Inn survive strange summer weather, the arrival of the new resort, *and* the start of a special relationship?

Getaway Bay (Book 2): Can Esther deal with dozens of business tasks, unhappy tourists, *and* the twists and turns in her new relationship?

Women's Beach Club (Book 3): With the help of her friends in the Beach Club, can Tawny solve the mystery, stay safe, and keep her man?

Straw and Diamonds (Book 4): Can Sasha maintain her sanity amidst their busy schedules, her issues with men like Jasper, and her desires to take her business to the next level?

The Billionaire Club (Book 5): Can Lexie keep her business affairs in the shadows while she brings her relationship out of them? Or will she have to confess everything to her new friends...and Jason?

Sweet Breeze Resort (Book 6): Can Gina manage her business across the sea and finish the remodel at Sweet Breeze, all while developing a meaningful relationship with Owen and his sons?

Rainforest Retreat (Book 7): As their paths continue to cross and Lawrence and Maizee spend more and more time together, will he find in her a retreat from all the family pressure? Can Maizee manage her relationship with her boss, or will she once again put her heart—and her job—on the line?

Getaway Bay Singles (Book 8): Can Katie bring him into her life, her daughter's life, and manage her business while he manages the app? Or will everything fall apart for a second time?

Turn the page to view series starters from three of my other series!

BOOKS IN THE GETAWAY BAY ROMANCE SERIES

Escape to Getaway Bay and meet your new best friends as these women navigate their careers, their love lives, and their own dreams and desires. Each heartwarming love story shows the power of women in their own lives and the lives of their friends.

The Island House (Book 1): Charlotte Madsen's whole world came crashing down six months ago with the words, "I met someone else."

Can Charlotte navigate the healing process to find love again?

BOOKS IN THE STRANDED IN GETAWAY BAY ROMANCE SERIES

Meet the McLaughlin Sisters in Getaway Bay as they encounter disaster after disaster...including the men they get stranded with. From ex-boyfriends to cowboys to football stars, these sisters can bring any man to his knees when the cards are stacked against them.

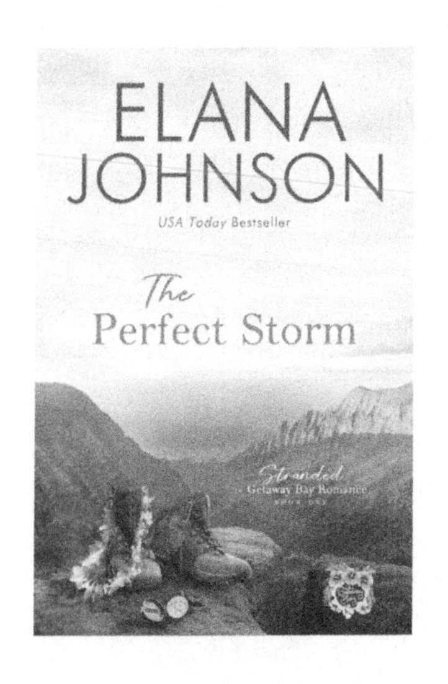

The Perfect Storm (Book 1): A freak storm has her sliding down the mountain...right into the arms of her ex. As Eden and Holden spend time out in the wilds of Hawaii trying to survive, their old flame is rekindled. But with secrets and old feelings in the way, will Holden be able to take all the broken pieces of his life and put them back together in a way that makes sense? Or will he lose his heart and the reputation of his company because of a single landslide?

BOOKS IN THE HAWTHORNE HARBOR ROMANCE SERIES

Escape to the beach today with single moms, single dads, and that one old lady that knows everyone in town... This sweet and clean romance series is sure to have the heartfelt love stories and heartwarming women's fiction you're looking for.

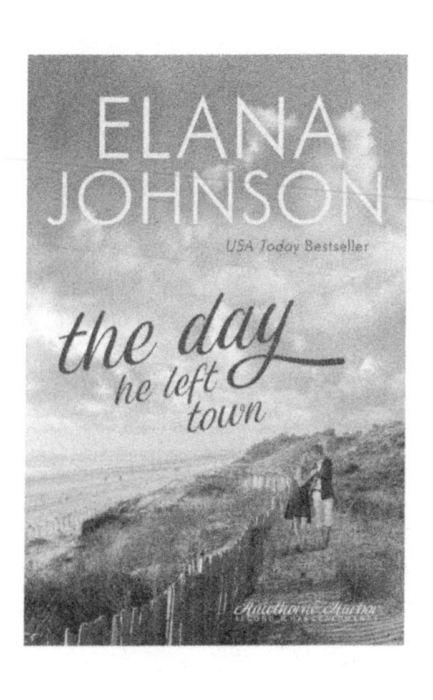

The Day He Left Town (Book 1): He's waiting for a promotion to come through. She's back in her hometown after a humiliating break-up. Can Tony and Cat make their second chance stick this time?

ABOUT ELANA

Elana Johnson is the USA Today bestselling and Kindle All-Star author of dozens of clean and wholesome contemporary romance novels. She lives in Utah, where she mothers two fur babies, works with her husband full-time, and eats a lot of veggies while writing. Find her on her website at feelgoodfictionbooks.com

Made in United States
North Haven, CT
28 December 2023

46720785R00157